THE NOTHING to see HERE
*** HOTEL ***

FIEND
of the
SEVEN SEWERS

STEVEN BUTLER

ILLUSTRATED BY STEVEN LENTON

SIMON & SCHUSTER

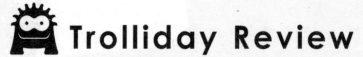

Trolliday Review

You are viewing user reviews for The Nothing To See Here Hotel, Brighton

The Nothing To See Here Hotel

NB. Everyone is welcome at The Nothing to See Here Hotel (except humans... NEVER HUMANS!)

👾👾👾👾👾 1,079 Reviews   #1 of 150 Hotels in Brighton

📍 Brighton Seafront UK BN1 1NTSH   📞 00 11 2 334 4556   ✉ E-mail hotel

---

Francesca Simon

👾👾👾👾👾 Reviewed 2 days ago

'A rip-roaring, swashbuckling, amazerous magical adventure. Comedy gold.'

Jeremy Strong

👾👾👾👾👾 Reviewed 13 days ago

'A splundishly swashbungling tale of trolls, goblins and other bonejangling creatures. Put on your wellies and plunge into the strangest hotel you will ever encounter. This is a hotel I hope I never find! Wonderfully, disgustingly funny.'

Cressida Cowell

👾👾👾👾👾 Reviewed 29 days ago

'Hilariously funny and inventive, and I love the extraordinary creatures and the one thirty-sixth troll protagonist...'

Trolliday Review

You are viewing user reviews for The Nothing To See Here Hotel, Brighton

The Nothing To See Here Hotel

NB. Everyone is welcome at The Nothing to See Here Hotel (except humans... NEVER HUMANS!)

1,079 Reviews   #1 of 150 Hotels in Brighton

Brighton Seafront UK BN1 1NTSH   00 11 2 334 4556   E-mail hotel

---

Liz Pichon

Reviewed 33 days ago

'This hotel gets five slimey stars from me...'

Jacqueline Wilson

Reviewed 54 days ago

'A magical hotel, known for its exclusive unique clientele. The chef is to be congratulated for inventing Bizarre Cuisine. All staff very friendly, but avoid the Manager (especially if you're wearing a cat-suit).'

Kaye Umansky

Reviewed 75 days ago

'What a fun hotel! Book me in immediately!'

WELCOME TO THE NOTHING to see HERE HOTEL

WELCOME TO

THE N⊕THING to see HERE HOTEL

Regurgita
Glump

Grottle
Glump

Rozomastrus
Bracegirdle

Grizhilda
Glump

Alfus
Chaff

Limina
Lightfoot

Lylifa
Glump

Crumpetra
Glump

Stodger
Banister

Ranis
Roy

Frankie
Banister

Abraham Banister

Olympia Nocturne

Zennifer Glump

Oculus Nocturne

Ignotius Glump

Tussely Banister

Blundus Glump

Festus McGurk

Bombastis Banister

Bargeous Banister

Markle Banister

The Banister Family Tree

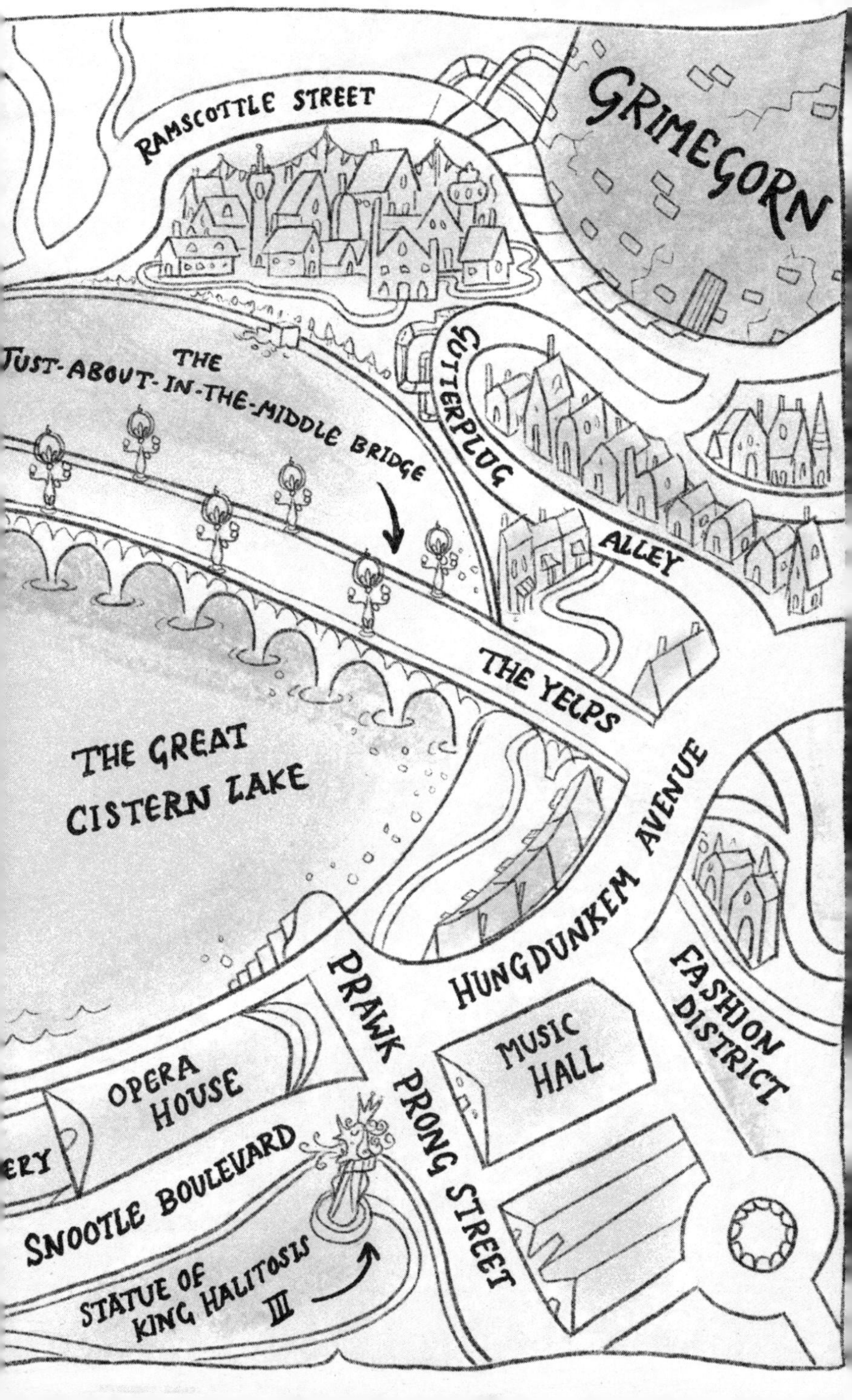
RAMSCOTTLE STREET
GRIMEGORN
THE
JUST-ABOUT-IN-THE-MIDDLE BRIDGE
GUTTERPLUG
ALLEY
THE YELPS
THE GREAT
CISTERN LAKE
HUNGDUNKEM AVENUE
PRAWK PRONG STREET
FASHION
DISTRICT
MUSIC
HALL
OPERA
HOUSE
ERY
SNOOTLE BOULEVARD
STATUE OF
KING HALITOSIS
III

WELCOME! **HOTEL** BRIGHTON, UK

THE NOTHING TO
SEE HERE HOTEL
Brighton S

MAGICALS WELCOME! **HOTEL** BRIGHTON, UK

THE NOTHING TO
SEE HERE HOTEL
Brighton Seafront
UK
BN1 1NTSH

Are you in need of a relaxing getaway or somewhere to escape the daily grind of lair lurking, bridge bothering or humdrum haunts? **The Nothing to See Here Hotel** is the place for you. We take honkhumptious pride in being the best secret holiday destination for magical creatures in the whole of England.

Whether it's soaking your scales in our pool, sampling the toothsome delicacies created by our spider-cook extraordinaire, Nancy (her porcupaties smothered in sticky giblet jam are to die for), reading up on a curse or two in the library, or just cooling your bunions at our luxurious mud spa, we guarantee there's something for everyone.

To confirm your booking, please fill in the attached form.

S **Here Hotel**, we'd be

ROOM SERVICE

'RUN, BANISTER BOY! FASTER!' Princess Viscera Von Tangle yipped with glee as we whizzed round another corner of the tenth-floor corridors. 'NOW, GO THIS WAY! AND THAT WAY! WOO-HOOOOO!'

I was pushing the old food trolley and sprinting as fast as I could, while Viscera was standing on top, clutching tightly onto a pair of salt and pepper shakers like a demented charioteer, whooping as we bumped along.

Of all the chores that Mum and Dad make me do around the hotel, delivering room service is definitely one of my new favourites, and not just because I get to clatter about the place with the wobbly wheeled trolley and an over-excited piskie princess.

After all the DISASTERS we've had here lately, knocking on all the doors and seeing what our weird and wonderful guests are getting up to in their rooms feels HONKHUMPTIOUS. And in a place like **The Nothing To See Here Hotel**, the UK's number-one holiday destination for magical creatures, you can bet your life that our customers aren't doing anything boring, like playing tiddlywinks or taking a nap or reading a long book.

Nope! Things are always bonkers around here. Weird is normal to my BRILLIANT family, let me tell you …

Just last week, Mum knocked on the door of room 357 with a bowl of snatchling steaks and was nearly washed all the way back to reception in a flash flood! The geriatric puddle-nymph who was staying in there wasn't in the mood to hobble down to the hotel pool and had decided to run all the taps, turning her bedroom into a luxury aquarium for one.

Dad was furious. It took him and our team of

home-sweet-home hobs an entire week to mop that mess up!

So …

Before we get stuck into the juicy bits of the story and in case we haven't met before, this is probably a good moment to tell you that my name is Frankie, Frankie Banister. Hello!

I know it sounds a bit loop-de-loop crazy, but I'm the sixth generation of the Banister/Bulches, a hugely-muddled bunch of humans and trolls, and all sorts of other magicals in between. I've stuck our family tree at the beginning of the book for you to have a look at, if you're feeling nosier than an armful of ogre bogeys.

Us lot have been living and working in **The Nothing To See Here Hotel** for well over one hundred years, ever since my great-great-great-grandad, Abraham Banister, fell in love with a honking brute of a troll, my great-great-great-granny, Regurgita Glump. They got married in a snog-a-lumptious ceremony down in the sewers under Brighton high street, and the rest is history. I swear I'm not fibbing!

A century later, Granny Regurgita still lives in the tallest tower of the hotel, and the ghost of Grandad Abe recently checked back in from the land of the dead to stay with us.

These days, the old spook mostly spends his time haunting the staircases and spouting romantic poetry to his warty wife while she's grumbling in bed. Granny absolutely hates it, but Abraham is convinced she's a total beauty-toot and won't give up trying to woo her.

Bleeuurrgh!

Now, I know this all sounds very strange indeed, but it's also very true – and if you haven't read any of my books before now, then you've got a whoppsy load of catching up to do.

This summer alone has seen underwater rollercoaster rides, goblin princes getting gobbled, screaming lawns, chicken-powered caravans, cursed dentures, skeleton mermaids, Trogmanay feasts ruined by marauding shrunken heads, whispering wallpaper, yetis arriving in a blistering blizzard, bones in a box, hypnotised ghosts, Arctic ulks, fountain statues springing to life … and that's only the boring bits.

I haven't even filled you in about my great-great-uncle, Oculus Nocturne, returning from oblivion and trying to destroy the hotel and all my family – TWICE!

I told you things were weird, huh?

But stick around for a few more pages and you'll see that it's all about to get a WHOLE lot weirder.

Don't panic! I know it's a lot to take in, but I can

catch you up on all the gory details of my BONKERS uncle and the rest of the craziness as we go along, I promise.

Anyway, where was I? Ah, yes … room service! Already that night we'd dropped off a platter of dung-beetle doughnuts to Old Gringus the pine dryad in room 276, three huge bowls of sugar lumps to the Molar Sisters in room 581, and a sizzling skillet of curried mud-whifflers with extra-spicy mango chutney to Gladys Potts the werepoodle in room 863.

'Where next, Viscera?' I panted as we rounded a bend so fast the food trolley nearly hit the wall.

'That's Princess Viscera to you, quarterling!' the tiny piskie snapped. 'The blunking cheekiness!'

'All right!' I huffed, rolling my eyes and secretly smiling to myself.

Ever since I'd rescued the princess at the bottom of the ocean and we'd made our escape from being eaten by a Gundiskump, I'd grown quite fond of

Viscera Von Tangle – although I wouldn't admit it to her. You see, there's no denying she's a snooty royal pain in the bumly-bits, but the tiny princess is actually lots of fun, especially when she comes along on the room-service rounds.

Watching her squawking orders like she's the most fearsome ruler in all the worlds, while holding on for her minuscule life between the salt and pepper, is rib-ticklish, if you ask me.

'Where next, your most excellent highness?' I tried again.

'Wait, impatient boy! Give me a second!' Viscera was standing on the piece of paper that Nancy, our giant spider-chef, had written all the deliveries, and she glanced down between her pea-sized feet to read for a moment.

'ROOM 1043!' she hollered in a voice barely louder than the trolley's rusty wheels. 'Squirrel-milk pancakes and a side of battered sea-cucumber nuggets. GO!'

With that, I rattled the trolley round the next corner of the hallway, and we swerved just in time to avoid crashing into Maudlin Maloney as she was coming out of the mud spa, muttering to herself.

'**GAH!!**' the ancient leprechaun shrieked, flailing her stumpy tattooed arms as she fell back against the door, sending her pet chickens flapping in all directions. 'What the **BLUNKERS** are you playin' at, you wee eejit?'

In her fluffy dressing gown covered in stains, with her ratty dreadlocks wrapped in a towel, Maudlin looked hilarious. It didn't help that she had a green seaweed slime-pack smeared all over her face.

'Umm ... you look wonderful, Maudlin!' I blurted, trying to think quickly and distract myself from giggling. 'Very fresh and rested.'

I'd have to be noggin-bonked to make fun of the grizzly old grunion at a time like this – or to stop running, for that matter. The tatty bad-luck fairy had been in a foul mood ever since her caravan-home had been grunched by the Gundiskump a few weeks ago, and even though Dad and our handyogre, Ooof, had built her a new cottage in the hotel gardens, she was still hopping mad and being a right grumpus about it.

'**THAT'S IT!** I've had it! I ought to hex the bejingles out of yer!' she squawked as we raced past. 'And that pimple of a princess too! Don't think I didn't spot you there, Viscera Von DUNGLE!'

'**Sorry, Maudlin!**' I yelled over my shoulder, trying to speed up and get out of sight round the next bend before she started dishing out her worst spells. Only two days ago Maloney had put a curse on the painting of my great-aunt, Crumpetra Glump, that hangs in the foyer, because she thought it was looking at her rudely. The dusty portrait sprouted carbuncles and oozed disgusting yellow gloop all the way down the wall above reception, and I certainly didn't want to suffer the same fate. 'Have a lovely evening!'

'You watch yourself, Frankie Banister!' I heard Maudlin yell behind me. 'You're not too old for a

smacked rump, donchaknow … and I smell trouble
in the air tonight! Trouble for you!!'

TROUBLE

'Done!' Viscera beamed, after we'd served the last plate of dinner to Reginald Blink. She looked up at me and grinned a mischievous grin. 'Now for the exciting part, Banister boy!'

'Let's go!' I cheered and pushed the cart back in the direction of the great staircase. All this running about delivering meals was totally worth it because of the ride back to reception. 'Hold on to your crown!'

I promise you, there is nothing more fun in the worlds than hopping on the back of the food trolley and clattering all the way down and around ten flights of spiral stairs to the ground floor below. The rusty old thing is under an enchantment to stop it from ever toppling over, so, no matter how rough

and rumbly the ride gets, we always make it down in one piece. And it's far better than walking. Haha!

Run, run, run … turn left!

Run, run, run … skid right!

We had almost reached the tenth-floor landing, when …

'FRANKIE!'

A yell-a-phone receiver buzzed on the wall next to us.

'FRANCIS BANISTER, ARE YOU THERE?'

It was Mum's voice. How did she always know exactly where to find me? If she wasn't completely human, I'd swear Mum had magical locating powers.

I looked down at Princess Von Tangle, who pulled a face and shrugged, then I stopped the trolley and walked nervously over to the trumpet-shaped contraption.

Mum and Dad only ever call me Francis when they're about to throw a wobbler and tell me off, so I knew this wasn't going to be good news on the other end.

'H-hello?' I said in my most 'WE HAVEN'T BEEN RACING WITH THE TROLLEY AGAIN' voice. 'Everything all right, Mum?'

'Francis!' Mum's voice barked up the pipes from the kitchen. I could practically hear her scrunching her nose in temper. She always does that when she's angry. 'I've just had Maudlin on the yell-a-phone telling me that you and Viscera nearly squashed her flat in the hallway!'

'No!' I said. 'It wasn't like that ...'

'What have I told you about speeding in the corridors, young man? Imagine if you'd actually crashed into Maloney, of all people. She'd hex the entire hotel in a heartbeat! We'd all be chickens! **CHICKENS WITH CARBUNCLES!'**

'I know, but ...'

'NO BUTS! Have you delivered all the room service?'

'Yep!' I said. 'It's all finished.'

'Good!' Mum snapped. 'Now get back down to the kitchen this instant, Francis, and don't you dare race that rusty cart about the place anymore. I mean it!'

The yell-a-phone line clicked and went dead. So much for having fun …

I groaned and turned back to Viscera, then slowly pushed the trolley across the landing to the top of the stairs.

'Right, hop off,' I said to the tiny piskie, holding out my hand for her to climb onto it. 'Let's go, Princess.'

Normally, once all the room-service deliveries are finished and I'm being well behaved, I press a tiny button on the side of the trolley handle and the whole thing shrinks and curls itself into a little metal disk the size of a giblet-jam-jar lid. It's a super handy bit of troll magic. That way I can pop it into my uniform pocket ready for next time.

'Shan't!' Viscera scowled up at me, then folded her arms. 'No!'

'Come on, we've got to get downstairs pronto or Mum's head will explode.'

'We can go much faster if we – ' she grinned and flicked her gaze in the direction of the stairs – 'if … we … travel … on …'

'We can't!' I half-gasped/half-whispered. 'We're already in a whoppsy load of trouble!'

'Exactly!' Viscera squeaked, pointing a tiny finger at me. Her eyes were wide with excitement. 'You're already in hot water … what's a bit more? I'm your ruler and I demand it. LET'S GO, BANISTER BOY!!'

3

MUM'S GONE WONKY

CRASH!!!

The trolley wheels hit the black and white tiles of the reception floor with an ear-splitting squeal, then skid right out into the middle of the room.

'Woo hoo!' Viscera yelped, letting go of the salt and pepper shakers and twirling about. 'That was our whooshiest one yet, I think.'

I opened my eyes and glanced about the foyer. It was mostly quiet. *Phew!*

Ooof was at the carved stone reception counter checking in a gaggle of scullery blights who were coming in to land on their rusted spoons and forks through an open window, and my great-great-aunt Zennifer had clomped and creaked down from her fountain-perch and was stretched out on a sofa, snoring.

'Hello, Frankie!' Ooof called with a toothy grin on his face. He waved one of his massive green arms and swatted an unfortunate scullery blight straight back out of the window. 'You very fast tonight!'

'Evening, Ooof!' I replied, feeling myself relax. Our handyogre would never tell Mum we'd been racing again, and my great-great-aunt Zennifer was a statue and couldn't speak. Apart from the family of impolumps we'd practically terrified to death as the trolley clattered around the staircase near the seventh-floor landing, I thought Viscera and I had got away with another terrific high-speed trolley dash.

'Well done, me hearty!' I growled to the little piskie princess in a voice like one of the heroes I'd seen in my *Adventures of Captain Plank* comic books. 'Another honkhumptious adventure.'

'I'm not your HEARTY!' she scoffed as she straightened her paperclip crown. 'I'm your leader, stupid quarterling!'

I rolled my eyes and smiled to myself, hopped off the back of the trolley and started pushing it in the direction of the hallway that led to the kitchens. We'd barely passed the empty fountain in the middle of the spiral floor, when ...

'Frankie, darling, can you come in here for a moment?'

It was Mum calling from the library. I stopped dead and felt the hairs prickle on the back of my neck.

Why was Mum in the library?

She must have rushed to reception and hidden to try and catch us in the act! There was no way she'd have missed us whizzing down the stairs with all the racket we were making.

'Oh, squits!' Viscera whispered. She folded her tiny arms and shook her head at me like I was the only one who'd disobeyed. 'You've been well and truly rumpled, Banister boy. There's going to be **BIG TROUBLE** for you.'

'Hurry, darling, it's important,' Mum's voice called again. 'Come, come …'

I pushed the trolley over to the library entrance, lifted Viscera down to the floor, then clicked the button on the metal handle. In an instant, the rickety cart twisted and shrank into a small metal disk and I tucked it into the front pocket of my jacket, where I keep my lucky piece of Gundiskump tooth and some folded photographs of my family.

'Good fortune, quarterling,' the princess squeaked as she peeked round the edge of the library archway.

I nodded down to the tiny piskie, then peered round the corner too.

'There you are, my little dove,' Mum said when she spotted me. 'I was waiting for such a long time.'

LITTLE DOVE?! Mum had never called me that in my life. Occasionally, if I've ever done something MEGA-naughty and Mum is about to explode like a muskrumple with measles, she has this super-secret mum-weapon where she pretends everything is absolutely fine. Then, just when I relax and think I'm not in hot water ... *ROAR! SCREAM! POINT! HUFF! BLARG!* I've been sent to my bedroom and I'm not allowed any seagull-snot ice cream with crumbly acorn topping after dinner for a week.

If Mum was calling me 'little dove', it looked like I was about to witness the biggest strop-wobbler of the century.

'Everything all right?' I stammered.

The library was completely dark and Mum was

standing with her back to one of the high-arched windows.

'What are you waiting for, silly?' she giggled. 'Come closer.'

I didn't move. Being a kid with troll-blood in my veins, I can see perfectly well when the lights are off, but the street lamps and the flashing glow of Brighton Pier outside meant I could only make out Mum's silhouette and … well … I couldn't quite put my finger on it, but something wasn't right. Her left shoulder was much higher than the right, and one of her feet was turned inwards.

It looked like the time Mum pulled a muscle lifting Hoggit, my pet pygmy soot-dragon, and she had to lie down on a pack of frozen pronglepeas from Nancy's freezer for days.

'Frankie,' Mum chuckled again. 'I said come here, you sweet thing. I've got a surprise for you.'

I still didn't move. A strange tingle of fear crept up my spine and I felt the urge to return to the reception desk and get Ooof to come into the library with me.

Glancing back to where Viscera had been standing near the archway, I saw she was now gone.

I should have known that stern little stropling would abandon me to get into trouble on my own.

'Frankie,' Mum cooed like she was singing a nursery rhyme. 'Come here.'

'Are you feeling okay?' I asked into the shadows. 'Why are you standing in the dark?'

'It's a secret. I have an early birthday present,' Mum's silhouette said. 'Me and Daddy took ages to pick it out. Don't you want it?'

A BIRTHDAY PRESENT!? Ha! So that's what all this was about. I practically laughed out loud thinking how stupid I was for getting all worried. It made perfect sense now. Honktober 31st was only a week away. No wonder Mum was sounding so weirdly nice. This had obviously been a trick to get me downstairs for the grand unveiling of my pre-birthday prezzie.

I hurried into the room, racking my brains for what it could be. I'd asked for a set of warp stones and a gravity-defying duvet cover so I could sleep on my bedroom ceiling. That would be **AMAZING** if my parents had actually got me—

When I was only two steps away from her, Mum lifted her head into the shaft of light pouring in through the window and … I … I … I felt my knees buckle and nearly toppled to the ground.

'AAGH—' I barely had time to muster the beginnings of a yelp before she clamped her hand over my mouth.

Something was terribly wrong! The thing in front of me was **NOT MY MOTHER**. She looked like Mum – sort of. All the parts of her face were present, but not quite in the right places, as if she was wearing a slightly rubbish mask.

'SHUT YOUR GOBBLE-GAP!' a gravelly voice croaked. Before my eyes, Mum twisted and distorted like a jellyfish in a blender. There was the sound of squelching and popping as a glimmer-spell was uncast, and the wonky woman suddenly transformed into two goblins, one standing on the shoulders of the other.

'SURPRISE, SNOTFACE!'

I opened my mouth to scream again, but the goblin at the top was holding a portable prattle-peacer. Great-Great-Great-Grandad Abraham had shown me one just like it when we visited his office in the Briny Ballroom at the bottom of the sea.

The goblin flicked the little device on and I watched in shock as my voice was instantly sucked out of my throat and into it like a wisp of smoke.

'That should do it,' the stumpy thing snickered. 'What's the matter, overling? Lost for words?'

With no way of crying out for help, I turned to run, but the larger goblin at the bottom was ready for me.

'Where'd you think you're going, grubling?' it barked, tossing a coil of golden rope from a hook on its belt. 'Not so fast!'

Instantly, the magical cord wrapped round my middle, lashing my arms to my sides and stopping me in my tracks. The goblins yanked on the end, dragging me back towards them.

'You can't beat a good bit of enchanted trap-lace for takin' prisoners, I say. That was easier than pokin' pluglets in a pie.'

I spun round and got my first proper look at the pair of squat attackers as they leered at me in the gloom. The smaller goblin at the top jumped down to the floor and sauntered towards me.

'That was exciterous!' she cackled. 'What now, Flott? Can we jab him in the ribblies?'

'No!' the larger goblin named Flott grunted, joining his accomplice. 'You know the rules.'

'Owww! How about just a few small wallops in the woo-woo?' the female goblin whined sulkily.

'We could boink him on the bonce!'

'Officer Lickspittle, you know our orders,' Flott huffed. 'No jabbing, walloping or boinking! The boss wants him unharmed.'

'Ugh!' Lickspittle huffed. 'FINE!'

My mind was racing so fast I thought I might faint. What was going on, and who was **THE BOSS?**

The lumpy creatures stepped further into the moonlight. They were an ugly pair, all right.

Flott was missing half an ear and had a shock of red hair tied in a knot on top of his knobbly green head. Lickspittle was wearing an eyepatch and her rusty locks were twisted in little wiry plaits that stuck out in all directions from her scalp like the upturned roots of a tree.

Both of them were dressed in smart soldiers' uniforms.

'Got you, you little skuz-lumper,' Lickspittle hissed next to my ear. 'You're in for it now.'

'Job done!' Flott said, coiling the loose end of the trap-lace round his hand and elbow. 'Let's be off.'

My brain was a swirl of panic and fear. I struggled against the golden cord, but it was clear I wasn't going anywhere fast. It seemed to be squeezing me tighter and tighter, the more I wriggled.

'The boss is going to be so pleased with us,' Lickspittle laughed, clapping her little hands. 'I bet we get medals for—'

'**FRANKIE!**' my real mum's voice suddenly called from reception behind us, making my heart leap into my silent throat. She must have wondered where I'd got to and come looking for me, ready to tell me off. 'Where is that boy? Ooof, have you seen Frankie?'

HOP IT! the taller goblin grunted. **NOW!**

I heaved against the enchanted cord round my middle, trying to stay put. Right this second, Ooof would be pointing to the library doors, and any moment now Mum would see me and raise the alarm.

'Don't even think about it, you stinkly human!' Lickspittle snarled. She flung the window wide open and before I even realised what was happening, the repulsive duo dragged me outside into the blustery night.

KIDNAPPED!

What did I tell you, my reader friend? I bet you could never have imagined in a squillion years at the beginning of this book that there was going to be a goblin kidnapping so soon, did you? You didn't think for a moment that I'd be getting swizzled straight from our own library?

Well, I was – and it was gut-gurglingly scary.

I swear, I'd never experienced anything stranger in all my life than having my voice stolen by some curious magical contraption. It was bonkers! I didn't once stop trying to holler as the goblins dragged me across the front lawn and along the pavement towards the pier, but absolutely no sound was coming out of my mouth. It was like hitting the silence button on the yell-a-phone when Dad was giving me a list of chores to do around the hotel.

Flott and Lickspittle hurried past the entrance to the aquarium with me stumbling behind. They might only have been as tall as my waist, but the goblins were stocky and brutish and much stronger than I was. I had no hope of stopping them – even when they ran **STRAIGHT OUT INTO THE ROAD!**

Cars braked and honked their horns, and one man on a bicycle veered off the pavement and zigzagged down onto the beach with a loud **CRUNCH**.

'Keep going!' Lickspittle huffed, ignoring the angry yelling and beeping. 'Nearly there!'

They hauled me closer and closer to the pier with its bright flashy lights and noisy amusements.

'You're insane,' I screamed silently at the back of their heads as we approached the entrance with all the colourful posters and the little clock tower on top. 'We'll be spotted!'

You see, even though it was a drizzly evening, tourists were still coming and going in their hundreds. Everywhere I looked there were families and children buying balloons and buckets of popcorn or playing on the games to win fluffy toys and shiny watches.

Any second now, some poor unsuspecting human would turn and see a quarterling child with pointy ears and eyes the colour of copper pennies being yanked along by a pair of gnarled-looking goblins. How could Flott and Lickspittle be so brain-boogled with this many people about?

I quickly got my answer as I spotted our shadows on the wobbly wooden walkway in front of us. Instead of the two goblin officers, I saw Mum's shape stretching out across the floor. The golden cord was still clutched in her shadow-hand, but instead of me at the end of it, there was the outline of a chubby little dog trotting along behind.

Those rottly gurnips had cast a glimmer on me too! Any humans who spotted us were just looking at a woman walking her pet pooch.

'This way,' Flott said as we hurried around the side of the great big arcade with 'BRIGHTON PALACE PIER' written on the front of it in huge sparkly letters, passing a row of food huts and jewellery stalls.

Where in the worlds were they taking me? I've walked up and down this place loads of times with Nancy in her magical disguise as a human-granny. Surely the goblins knew it was a dead end? If we kept going, we'd eventually fall into the sea!

'Just over here …'

By now we were about halfway along the pier, and we stopped outside a green painted caravan with a rounded roof and little steps leading up to the front door. It looked a bit like the one Maudlin Maloney had lived in (before it got grunched by the Gundiskump), only this one was human-sized and much bigger. There was a large sign on the side of it advertising fortune-telling and predictions in;

Career, Love, Happiness and Luck.

'This is it,' Lickspittle snorted excitedly. She turned to me and grinned. 'Oooh, you're in such a bundle of bother, whelping!'

I don't think I could have been more confused if I tried. Had this repugnant pair stolen me from my home and brought me all the way out here in the cold to get my palms read?

The two goblins made for the caravan, pulling me behind them, but just when I thought they were going to head up the steps at the front, they ducked underneath it, vanishing into the shadows behind the spoked wheels.

'GET A MOVE ON, QUARTERLING!'

I had to shuffle under on my knees, which was made a lot trickier by the fact my arms were still tied to my sides.

'Shift your shufflies,' Lickspittle snapped at me in a whisper and yanked me further into the gloom. 'Lazy little lumper!'

By now, I didn't know how to feel. My belly was gurgling with that horrible gloopy feeling I get right before something terrible happens – don't forget, stuff like this isn't altogether uncommon when you live at **The Nothing To See Here hotel** – but I also had the tiniest tingle of curiosity as I watched the bigger goblin knock on the wooden boards beneath us and a square trapdoor opening upwards, pushed by a long-fingered furry hand.

'In you go, you gunksome little skwonker,' Lickspittle said. Then she booted me right in the bumly-bits and I fell head first into the hole, screaming a silent scream.

THE GATEKEEPER OF BRIGHTON PIER

The last thing I expected to see when I opened my eyes after hitting a hard floor with a painful **HUMPH!** was a small dusty office, piled to the rafters with papers and scrolls.

I was lying on a little round rug, woven out of old fishing nets, that smelled of brine.

'Welcome, weary travellers,' an unfamiliar voice wheezed, snapping me back to my senses. 'Welcome, all.'

Slowly I wriggled onto my back and found myself staring up at the open trapdoor in the ceiling. Around me stood my two goblin attackers, plus a third, much older creature with bristly whiskers and a clay pipe sticking out from between its teeth.

I gulped when its wide yellow eyes met my gaze through its enormous spectacles. It was a mumpie! I'd come across pictures of these ancient wisdom-imps in Grandad Abe's books, but I'd never seen one in the flesh. They can normally be found minding their own business in the darkest recesses of old libraries and museums, as they live entirely on a diet of handwritten notes and letters. So what was this creature doing under Brighton Pier?

'Interesting …' the old mumpie rasped as it peered down at me. He raised a tufty eyebrow, then took the pipe out of his mouth with one of his four hands and scratched his head with the long mouthpiece. 'I'm not sure anyone's going to want to buy the likes of him, you know. Stinks of human! No one will eat that.'

'We're not here to sell the boy, Bambus!' Lickspittle laughed.

'He's got business with the boss,' Flott joined in.

THE BOSS? In all the chaos of being dragged along the pier, I'd forgotten about this mysterious character for a moment or two. Who was it? Who hated me enough to steal me away? My horrible pair of kidnappers might have been goblins, but they couldn't be working for Grogbah, surely? He'd be back at the hotel right now, moaning and whining as always. The last time I saw that royal whinge-bucket, Grogbah was complaining that he kept falling straight through the sun-loungers by the pool.

Then there was Maudlin. She might have been in a fumerous temper, but I didn't think she'd go to this much trouble. Besides, she'd NEVER associate with the likes of Flott and Lickspittle. Maudlin **HATED** underlings!

The only person left was my great-great-uncle. He couldn't be the boss, could he?

'Oh, blunkers!' The mumpie flinched with surprise. He hobbled around the stacks of papers to the other side of his cluttered desk. 'We'd better get you sorted, then.'

The goblin guards hauled me to my feet and shoved me closer to the mumpie as he busied himself, grabbing forms and folders from various drawers. There was a small sign at the front of his workstation that said, 'BAMBUS BOATSWIG: M-T-T-T GATEKEEPER AND BORDER CONTROL OFFICER'.

Gatekeeper of what? There was nowhere to go! I racked my brains but couldn't even begin to think what M-T-T-T might stand for.

'Right,' Bambus mumbled, snorting out a cloud of foul-smelling smoke. 'You two first. Travel permits, please!'

The goblin officers both reached inside their uniforms and produced little folded booklets.

'Look at your picture!' Lickspittle shrieked, pointing to Flott's permit as he opened it. 'Haha! Your hair!'

'It was taken a long time ago,' Flott muttered, his green cheeks flushing pink. 'It was fashionable at the time.'

They handed their booklets to Bambus, and the old mumpie stamped them one by one with a loud clunking contraption that looked a bit like a stapler.

'That's that,' the mumpie croaked as he turned his watery old eyes on me. 'Now, then, how about you, boy?' He reached under the desk and pulled out a thick and tatty tome with crinkled, browning pages.

Opening the book with a laboured grunt, Bambus snatched a seagull feather quill from an ink pot on a nearby shelf and poised his hand, ready to write.

'Name?' he said, eyeballing me suspiciously.

I opened my mouth to talk but nothing came out.

'Name, boy? I need your name!'

'He's been prattle-peaced,' Flott said. 'Gob-stoppered.'

'I see,' Bambus grumbled, peering at me over the top of his glasses. 'Well, I have to put something in the logbook or your journey ends here.'

'Ummm … His name is Disgusting Human Stink-Child the Eleventh!' Officer Lickspittle cooed. She jabbed me in the ribs with her pudgy finger, then looked guiltily at Flott, who shook his head at her.

'Dis … gusting … Human … Stink … Child …' Bambus mumbled to himself as he wrote the words into his register, 'the … Eleventh …'

He glanced back at me and fixed me in his ancient glare.

'Age?'

'I dunno,' Lickspittle said. 'He can't be that old.'

'SEVENTY-TWO!' Officer Flott blurted.

'Yep! That's probably about right,' Officer Lickspittle agreed. 'Seventy-two!'

The mumpie wrote these things down without questioning. So much for being a wisdom-imp!

'Purpose of visit?' he asked, still puffing on his pipe.

'Some good eatin' – if there's time,' Lickspittle answered, patting her paunch. 'I like the pickled gerbil tails from the market. I've always wanted to visit the Belcharium as well …'

'NO, YOU PLONKLE!' Officer Flott humphed at his partner. 'We're taking the boy to the boss for armfuls of vicious revenge. Great spiky loads of it!'

I swear, if my blood could have actually turned to ice, it would have at that moment. I couldn't even begin to understand what was going on. Who wanted revenge on me? I was only a kid!

I tried my absolute hardest to stop myself, but the more I thought about it, the more an image of my great-great-uncle, Oculus Nocturne, crept into my mind. What if … What if he'd escaped his ice prison in the Himalayas and was employing these two barnacle-bonces to come and capture me? It wouldn't be the first time he'd used brainless goblins to do his dirty work.

Oculus's living-ghost, a spectril, was in a jar on the top shelf of our library back at the hotel, and he was powerless without it. If the blighter had somehow escaped, it would be the first thing he'd come searching for.

I grimaced when I thought of the horrible things my uncle might do to make me tell him where it was.

THWACK!

I immediately snapped out of my thoughts as Bambus Boatswig slammed an enormous stamp, with lots of swirly runes on it, down onto the register page.

'That's all of you sorted,' he said with a satisfied smile. 'Officers Flott and Lickspittle, and … umm … Disgusting Human Stink-Child the Eleventh, on behalf of M-T-T-T… the Board of Magical Tourists, Travellers and Trippers, I grant the three of you safe passage into Hovel.'

Bambus yanked on a lever next to his desk and there was a great jolt that rattled us right down to the bones. The whole office shook and the sound of grinding gears filled our ears as the wall behind us started to slide slowly away with a mind-shattering metallic squeal.

HOVEL

I turned and gawped as the back of the room rattled aside and my head nearly rocketed off my shoulders with shock.

Now, let me just remind you one last time that I've lived in the hotel my whole life, and I've looked at Brighton Pier every single whoppsy day of it.

Anyone who has ever laid eyes on the pier knows that underneath the wooden boardwalk, the rides, the flashing signs and the noisy arcades there's … well … nothing! Nothing at all, except thousands of long metal struts that the entire thing sits on top of to keep it high above the water. Right?

WRONG!!

Before us, nestled amongst the iron legs above

the churning sea, sprawled a ... a ... a town! I swear I'm not fibbing! You have my permission to throw this book in the bin and never read one of my stories again if it turns out I'm lying to you, my reader friend.

I stood there twitching in startled silence as a dizzying mixture of pant-wetting fear and exhilaration fizzed in my brain. I was looking at an **ENTIRE TOWN** packed with magicals dashing this way and that!

'Move!' Flott grunted. I struggled against him, but the stocky goblin grabbed me by the elbows and shoved me out onto a small landing beyond the confines of Bambus's office walls.

'Enjoy your stay,' the old mumpie called behind us. 'If you get a chance, pop into Blubber McGonk's bakery. Her crustacean cakes and barnacle buns are to die for!'

With that, Bambus gave the lever a second tug and the wall clunkered back into place, leaving the three of us alone on the arrivals platform.

'There we go,' Flott said with a contented sigh

like all the hard work was over. He turned to his partner-in-crime and nodded. 'We're safely inside the obscuring spells. Should be fine to give the whelpling his voice back.'

'Righty!' replied Lickspittle. She fumbled in her pocket for the prattle-peacer.

'You can wail and gnash as much as you like now, boy,' Flott continued, grinning a spiteful grin at me. 'It won't make any difference. No human in the outside world can see or hear you.'

Lickspittle aimed the portable contraption in my direction and fiddled with it clumsily. There was a small click as the top opened and a wisp of white smoke wafted towards my face.

No sooner had I inhaled my voice back through my mouth and nostrils, I turned to my stumpy kidnappers and said …

'THIS IS AMAZING!'

The two goblins looked about as baffled as I was. I hadn't meant to shout that. I was practically weeping with worry, and what I wanted to say was, *'LET ME GO!'* or *'WHO ARE YOU?'* or *'BOG*

OFF!' but I was so surprised by the view, I couldn't help myself.

'There's a magical town hidden in Brighton?' I yelped.

'It's not Brighton!' Lickspittle snapped as she pulled a face like she was completely disgusted. 'It's Hovel, actually!'

'I can't believe I didn't have a clue about this place. How long has it been here? Where are we?'

'We should get a wriggle on,' said Flott, ignoring my questions. He yanked on the golden cord round my middle. 'I don't want to keep the boss waiting. It ain't right to test his patience.'

Aaaaand that was that ... My instant excitement was extinguished as I remembered that I'd been kidnapped and was being dragged off to meet a mystery stranger who wanted some kind of revenge.

'Let's go, pukeling – off to your **DOOM! TRA-LA-LA!**' Lickspittle cooed as she joined Flott, pulling me to the edge of the platform and down a dilapidated flight of stairs.

'**NO!**' I hollered, tugging against the rope

again. 'Please! You can't do this!'

'Yes, we can,' Flott teased. 'We already have.'

'Who's the boss?' I shouted. 'What does he want with me?'

'You'll find out,' Lickspittle teased. 'He's been DYING to see you.'

Dying to see me? Was this grizzly little goblin trying to give me clues? The image of my deathly uncle flashed through my mind again and I felt my knees go weak and juddery.

'I know hundreds of magicals!' I cried, racking my brains for an idea of how to stop them. 'There's bound to be someone here who'll recognise me, and then you'll be in so much trouble when they report you. My granny will squash you flat!'

Lickspittle burst out laughing.

'Someone from **The Nothing To See Here Hotel** visiting a town like this? You must be noggin-bonked!' she jeered. 'Hovel ain't the kind of place for poshly pooks and snooty snipes.'

'S'right,' Flott agreed with glee. 'You won't find any of those doff-doff-types around here, boy. This

is a squeery port for the bad'uns and brandy-
snatchers of the widely worlds. It's a proper rot-
nest. Now, shut your mumble-hole before we snuffle
your voice again!'

The goblins led me to the foot of the steps and
into a bustling street. I half-screamed, half-cheered
at the sight of Hovel in the light of hundreds of
lanterns that hung from the underside of the pier
above.

Ahead of us, ramshackle buildings with skewed
rooftops and bent chimney pots were snuggly
packed in and around the metal struts that criss-
crossed the way ahead like flies in a spider's web.
There were narrow wonky walkways winding in all
directions, and I could see the waves rumbling
below us through the gaps. Rickety staircases and
ramps led to other levels of the town beneath this
one, and everything creaked and groaned like a
banshee with bellyache.

'Keep up, boy,' Flott grunted as he dragged me
along. 'No more griping.'

'Ow!' I winced. The trap-lace was too tight and

now it was pinching me repeatedly in the ribs. It felt like something was digging around inside my pocket. It must have been the coiled-up room-service trolley or my lucky piece of Gundiskump tooth.

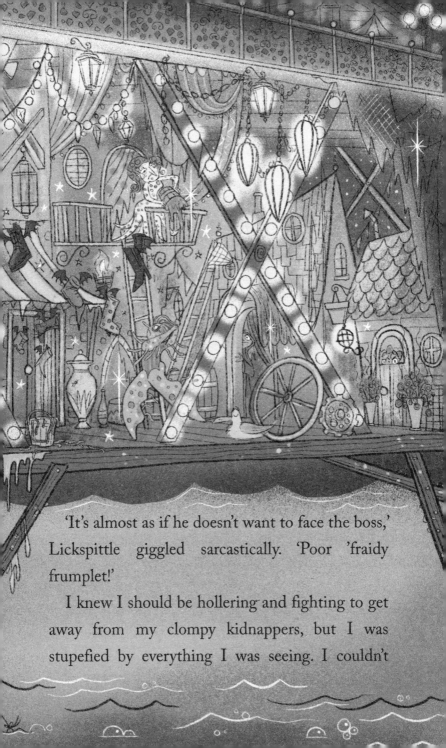

'It's almost as if he doesn't want to face the boss,' Lickspittle giggled sarcastically. 'Poor 'fraidy frumplet!'

I knew I should be hollering and fighting to get away from my clompy kidnappers, but I was stupefied by everything I was seeing. I couldn't shake off this bonkers excited feeling that prickled the hair on the back of my neck and gurgled my belly as more of the town came into view, and I secretly wished I had Dad's battered old camera with me.

Stumbling through the crowd of magicals going about their business, I couldn't help thinking about how much Great-Great-Great-Grandad Abraham would love to see this place. We'd spent loads of time together, reading about the hundreds of magically hidden towns dotted all over the world, but I'd never imagined there was one right under our noses.

All around, snarkles and kulpies and grumplings of all shapes and sizes were clomping back and forth, hurrying from one limpet-covered place to another with carts and sacks filled with things to buy and sell.

'WHAT THE CLONKERS IS THAT!?' A haggered bogrunt with a basket of sundried starfish on its back recoiled in horror when we crossed his path and he clapped eyes on me. **'IT'S 'ORRIBLE!'**

'Mind your mumbles,' Lickspittle shot back. 'Go stick your snout in someone else's business!'

As we made our way further into the throng, we passed clamorous restaurants that belched out clouds of spice-scented steam and bustling emporiums overflowing with arguing, bartering magicals. I tried my best to memorise the painted signs on the shopfronts in case I could escape and find my way back, but it was a blur of activity.

I spotted Gimble and Gump's Otherworldly Supplies, where Maudlin Maloney's skell-a-phone key had originally come from. I couldn't believe the old leprechaun hadn't told me the shop was right here underneath the pier! Its grubby windows were filled with weird and wonderful enchanted objects that even Flott and Lickspittle seemed fascinated by. The three of us had to duck as a flock of assorted old leather boots with bat wings came flapping out of the dingy front door, followed by an angry anemononk shopkeeper.

'Get back 'ere!' it gurgled, waving a net in the air as it slopped and squidged after the frantic swarm.

'I said "LACED" not "CHASED"!!'

I can't recall everything we came across – there was just too much to take in – but I do remember Old Mother Gnattle's Jellied Skrunts and Pies, Loonswagger's Human Junk, Effluenza Jangle's Tackle Shop and Plonk & Fisps Flowers, with its vases of rancid-looking sea sprouts outside.

At the end of the street, we walked into a market square filled with food stalls that was even more crowded than the row of shops.

It was a dizzying sight, as busy as the inside of a beehive. Hundreds of intoxicating smells filled my senses and made me feel giddy – and HUNGRY!

'ROASTED UNICORN! GET IT WHILE IT'S CRISPY!'

'TERMITE TACOS WITH SWAMP GRASS SALSA!'

'THE FINEST RAT-MILK CHEESES — FRESH FROM FRENCH SEWERS!'

In the middle of the open square was a roaring fire, and bubbling above it was the largest cauldron of glow-worm gumbo I'd ever seen. It was nearly as big as one of the swelky tanks back at the hotel, and a team of snub-nosed garvils were wobbling about at the top of ladders, stirring it with long wooden spoons like oars.

'Ooooh, smells delunktious.' Lickspittle beamed, patting her stomach. 'Can we get some? I want to try boiled badger burgers!'

'Not now, you dungle!' Flott snapped back at her. He pointed to the far side of the heaving square. 'We've arrived. Look!'

I squinted my eyes, trying to see what my goblin captor was gesturing at through all the cooking smoke, then gasped.

There, crammed between Spindle & Grubber's Salted Sluggery and Archibus Gulp's Fetchly Fashions, was the wrecked remains of a huge galleon. It hung between the metal joists of the pier at a crooked angle like some enormous wave had just washed it into position, and the carved figurehead on the front of the bow clutched an ornate brightly coloured sign.

'Here we are, boy.' Flott smirked with an ugly sneer as we stumbled across the uneven boards towards it.

Stopping beneath the figurehead, I glanced up to look at the scrolled writing between her scaly mermaid fingers. I was about to read it out loud, when the wooden sea-maiden twisted her head with a noisy cracking sound and smiled down at us.

'All right, dearies!' she bawled in a cockney accent, baring a set of rotten teeth that were mostly barnacles and winkle shells. 'Welcome to the Itchy Urchin pub. Come inside and whet your wumples!'

THE ITCHY URCHIN

'You've found the right place, me duckies!' the mermaid rasped with a grin. She shook her wooden locks, releasing a shower of splinters and the odd startled hermit crab. 'We've got the tastiest grub to help warm those aching bones, and the gluggliest grog in all of Hovel. You'll be blipsy in no time, you will. Try for yourself, darlings … Limpet Lil wouldn't lie to you.'

'We don't need any of your tourist twaddlesnipe, Lil!' Officer Flott grumbled at the pouting mermaid.

'Oh, stuff o' nonsense! I'm sure I don't know what you're chattywagging on about,' Lil giggled, doing her best to look shocked. 'Twaddlesnipe indeed! This here's the finest pub in all the slopsy seas.'

'Yeah, yeah, we know!' Lickspittle groaned. 'You do this every time we're here … same old jabbering.'

'I say,' Lil huffed. 'The rudeness! I don't jabber; it's my job! I'll have you know I'm the best welcome-wench this side of the Bermuda Triangle. I've got a certificate!'

Just then, the mouldy mermaid caught sight of me and cooed excitedly.

'Oh, a new face!' She smiled, almost dropping her wooden sign. 'Who's this one? Looks a bit young to be on the blowfish brandy.'

'He's no one,' Lickspittle answered. 'Just a …'

'I'M FRANKIE BANISTER!' I yelled over the goblin girl, shooting her an angry glare.

'Well, I never!' Lil exclaimed, leaning forward to get a better look at me. 'I know you, boy. Heard plenty of gossiping and chittery-chirping about that fancy hotel you're from, I have. What's it like? Is it as plushly as they say?'

The figurehead opened her mouth to ask more questions, but Flott raised his stumpy green hand and stopped her.

'The boy is expected … by the boss,' he said. 'Now …'

'Oh, good grumptious!' Limpet Lil flinched. Was it me, or did I see a flash of fear spread across her cracked face? 'You'd better go inside. He's been waiting a long time.'

With that, the mermaid tucked the sign under one arm and wriggled her driftwood fingers towards the rotten hull of the ship beneath her.

For a second nothing happened until, with an ear-splitting creak, it started to buckle and warp. Before our eyes, the wooden boards bent outwards, exposing a doorway just wide enough to walk through.

'What have you been up to, Frankie Banister?' the mermaid whispered as the goblins pulled me through the jagged opening. Her eyes were wide and worried. 'You must've done something awful!'

Inside, the Itchy Urchin was no quieter than the

square we'd just left, and the sound of barking market traders was replaced by the roar of music and laughter.

At any other time, I would have loved to spend the evening in a corner of the dimly lit pub, creature watching. Everywhere I looked, the round barrel-tables were crowded with merry magicals clinking tankards of frog grog and popping the corks on bottles of fizzy razorweed wine.

There was a small stage with three impolumps dancing and singing jazzy songs, accompanied by an octopus who played lots of bizarre instruments all at once. The poster nailed to the wall behind them said they were 'The McCrumple Brothers and Eight-armed Nev'.

'Get a move on!' Flott snarled as he dragged me over to the counter where a burley goblin bartender in a stained dress and apron was pouring drinks. She looked up at the two officers and nodded to them, as if to say, *I know exactly why you're here.*

Before either of my captors even spoke, the tattooed goblinette eyed me up and down and mumbled that 'He' was in the back booth, behind the curtain.

'Now you're in for it,' Lickspittle laughed between slurpy mouthfuls of plorkle scratchings. She'd sneakily snatched a bag of the disgusting things from an unsuspecting reveller as we crossed the pub. 'The boss is finally going to get his revenge and you'll be popped like a boil on a bog-bonker's backside.'

I didn't know what to do. I felt like I was somewhere between bursting into tears and wetting myself, as the grizzly pair hauled me to the far side of the galleon, where a green curtain was hung across a dark alcove in the shadows.

'Oh-ho-ho, this is going to be good,' Flott

chuckled. 'Proper thumpus!'

We stopped in front of the threadbare drape and I could hear hushed voices behind it. My knees started to shake and a swooshy feeling bubbled up into my throat as I prepared to look into the sickly green eye of my evil great-great-uncle again. It couldn't be anyone else, surely?

One thing was certain … only Oculus hated me enough to do something like this, and the more I thought about it, the more I was starting to panic.

I couldn't imagine how in the worlds he could have escaped his ice-block jail when the Kwinzi family of yetis were guarding it, but he'd done it nonetheless, and I was going to pay the price. My family had imprisoned Oculus in the Himalayas and locked his spectril up in a jar, after all. He was going to be **FURIOUS!**

'I think it's time you said hello to the boss,' Flott said. 'Smile!'

With that, the stumpy goblin yanked one half of the curtain aside and Lickspittle shoved me through the gap with a cackle of glee.

THE BOSS

I staggered into the gloom of the private booth, clamping my eyes shut before I caught sight of my **TERRIBLE** relative.

Without my arms to steady me, I sprawled straight across the table on the other side of the curtain, clattering plates and cutlery in all directions. When I finally came to a stop with my cheek squashed against the rough wood and the air knocked out of my chest, my blood was turning to ice in my veins.

'Please!' I yelped, without looking up. 'I'm just a kid! You don't need to do this, uncle. We're family! There must be another way! We don't have to spend the rest of our lives fighting …'

'I'M NOT YOUR UNCLE, YOU

RANCIDEROUS RUMPLET!' a familiar and whiny voice scoffed somewhere above me.

I opened one eye …

'I told you Frankie Banister was a clunkered brainburp!' the voice continued. 'Humans are **SO** stupidly!'

Holding my breath, I felt the terror in my stomach suddenly turn to anger as I stared down at the wet tabletop.

'Get up and look at me when I'm talking to you, **BANISTUMP!** I can't have my skudderous revenge if you don't oogle me in all my gruzzly glory, can I?'

'GROGBAH!' I yelled, scrambling back to my feet. 'What the BLUNKERS do you think you're doing?'

I stood up as straight and tall as I could with the rope still tied round my middle and scowled at the pumpkin-sized goblin-ghost. For a second, I thought I might sob with relief that it wasn't Uncle Oculus. After all this, it had just been another one of Grogbah's stupid tricks.

'Tremble in fear!' Prince Grogbah commanded in a voice like someone swinging on a rusted gate. He was floating just above the table with an excited grimace on his piggy little face.

'You scared me, you rotten pimple!' I hollered. 'I'm going to tell Mum and Dad!'

'PIMPLE!' Grogbah squealed in shock. **'YOU DARE TO CALL ME, THE HEIR TO THE DARK AND DOOKY DEEP, PIMPLE?'**

'Yes! Pimple!' I growled, half-expecting to see flames shooting from my nostrils. 'Pimple! Pimple! **PIMPLE!!** And you're not the heir to the dark and dooky deep any more. You're just a wafty-whiney spook!'

'Lies!'

'You popped your clonkers, remember?' I shouted, then winced in pain again. Whatever was in my pocket was really digging itself into my ribs beneath the enchanted golden cord.

'AAAAGH!' shrieked Grogbah, before sticking his scaly tongue out at me. 'You'll regret that, skunkus!'

'Mum is going to go BONKERS when she hears about this,' I continued, ignoring the goblin's threats. 'You'll be lucky if she doesn't suck you up into the vacuum cleaner like a dust pook's dinner!'

I honestly don't think I'd ever felt so angry in my whole life before that moment in the Itchy Urchin pub. I was HOPPING MAD and would have flicked the little gonker on the end of his bulbous nose if he hadn't already been made from smoke and fog.

You see, ever since Prince Grogbah came to hide out at **The Nothing To See Here Hotel** at the beginning of the summer and ended up getting grunched by Mrs Venus, he's caused no end of chaos.

In case you don't already know, it was GROGBOG who led Oculus Nocturne to the hotel in the first place and plotted to expose all of us magicals to the human world. We could have ended up in a zoo!

When plans didn't go well and Oculus was defeated, the chunksome goblin-ghost decided to haunt my bedroom instead and has been delighting in playing tricks and being a right pain in the bumly-bits whenever he can.

He's forever hiding my things, or pestering Hoggit, or turning my breakfast glass of junkumfruit juice into horrible gloopy ectoplasm when I'm not looking … but he'd never done anything this crazy before.

'You're in **SO MUCH TROUBLE!**' I said, remembering that only a few weeks ago, Maudlin Maloney had sworn to catch Grogbah in a potion bottle and flush him down the loo if he didn't stop being such an irritating snizzler. 'You won't get away with this.'

'Nonkumbumps!' Grogbah blurted, floating downwards until his potato-nose was almost touching mine. 'I'm not the one in a poodly amount of bother, Banister. You are!'

I'm happy to admit right here and now there are squillions of things that scare me, my reader friend, but a whiney little twerp of a goblin-ghost was not one of them. Well, not until tonight, but I'd never tell him that.

'I can't believe you made Flott and Lickspittle call you the boss!' I laughed, trying to sound as mocking as possible. 'As if a skrunt like you could ever be the boss of anything ...'

'I'M NOT THE BOSS!' Grogbah interrupted me again.

'What?' This was getting very confusing.

'I said ...' the ghost sneered, 'I'm not the boss, I'm Prince **BLUNKING** Grogbah. I don't do scuffly boss-work. I'm far too fancy-floofy for that!'

'W-well, who is it, then?' I stammered, feeling more perplexed by the second. The familiar swoosh of fear instantly bubbled back into my belly. If Grogbah wasn't the person I'd been brought here to see, there was a chance my uncle might still be looking for revenge. 'Is ... is ... is Oculus back?'

'Haha!' Grogbah pointed at me and howled. 'Frankie-Trembly-Trunks thinks his uncle's out to get him. **Woooooooooaaah!'**

'Who am I supposed to meet?' I yelled. **'WHO?'**

'That would be me ...'

I jolted with alarm as an unexpected and very gruff voice spoke in the shadows.

With all the muddle of being shoved through the green curtain and coming face to face with the lumpish face of Prince Grogbah, I'd failed to notice a second goblin sitting in the alcove.

'Now I've got your attention,' he rasped, before rocking his chair back, crossing his arms behind his head and clomping his booted feet onto the table. 'Do you know who I am, boy?'

'No,' I said.

The corner of this new goblin's eye twitched and the edges of his mouth curled downwards. Clearly, he thought I should know who he was.

'You should be quiverin' in your wimbly-pimbly little human panty-bloomers, in the presence of the boss,' the goblin continued. 'Allow me to introduce myself properly.'

I watched with wide eyes as the creature gulped down the last of his goblet of grog, stood up and swaggered towards me.

The boss was a beast of a thing – as tall as I was, which is practically unheard of for a Barrow Goblin, and twice as wide. He was wearing a similar uniform to Flott and Lickspittle, except his was blood red and every bit of it was covered in shiny medals and decorations. He was also sporting the curliest moustache I'd ever seen.

'Tell him, boss!' Lickspittle cheered with her head stuck through the curtain. 'I love this part!'

'I am Captain Pugnacious Grumpwhistle,' the goblin barked as he reached my side of the table. He grabbed a metal helmet that had been hooked on the back of a chair and plonked it on his head with a dull **CLOMP**.

I didn't know what to do, so I just stared silently.

'Didn't you hear me, boy?'

'He's Pugnacious Grump—' Flott and Lickspittle began in unison.

'Yes, thank you, you two!' Captain Grumpwhistle cut them off. 'I can do me own introductions!'

He paused for a moment and straightened out a wrinkle on the cuff of his uniform.

'... Commander of the Royal Guard of Barrow Goblins. Baron of Battles, Squasher of Scrumplets ...'

I still didn't know what to do or say, so I carried on staring.

'...**Clouter of Clamlies, Knocker of Ninkumpoopers**...'

I shook my head. What did this brute of a goblin want with me? I could understand why Grogbah might seek revenge, but I'd never even met Captain Grumpwhistle before. He had no reason to want to squish me!

'...**Destroyer of Dungles, Brute of the Brine Beds**...'

Grumpwhistle was clearly starting to get annoyed that I didn't know who he was and he glanced at Grogbah for support.

'Tell him why you're here,' the ghost-prince squealed with excitement. 'Go on!'

'I have official commands to snitch you away and bring you to the court of—' Grumpwhistle began.

'Banister boy thought we were in cahoots with that jangle-moaner, Oculus Nocturne!' Grogbah guffawed, cutting in. 'You wish, dungle brain!'

'Snitch you away and bring you to the court of—' the goblin commander tried again, but Grogbah interrupted once more.

'He's come to take you to someone far scarier than Oculus-One-Eyed Whinger-Nocturne!'

'And bring you to the court of …' Captain Grumpwhistle tried a third time, shooting a threatening glare at the spook-prince.

Grogbah spotted the angry look and mimed zipping his wonky mouth shut.

'… the court of …'

'QUEEN LATRINA!' Grogbah whooped,

spinning in circles and clapping his tiny hands. He floated back down until his nose was almost touching mine again. 'My moomsie wants a serious word with you …'

ONE LAST LOOK ...

I don't remember too much about who spoke or what happened next, my reader friend. My head felt like someone had reached inside and swizzled my brains up with an egg whisk.

Before I had time to run or cry or make my escape, I was dragged through a back door of the Itchy Urchin pub and down a narrow staircase, which descended steeply to a rickety wooden jetty, bobbing about on the breaking tide.

I'm sure Grogbah would have been cheering and hooting as he floated about, loop-de-looping around us, but the only sound I could hear was my nervous heart thumping in my ears.

You see, I'd read about Queen Latrina in books with Grandad Abe, but it's very easy to forget these things aren't just fairy tales and scary bedtime stories. If those dusty old tomes in the hotel library were telling the truth, she was a **TERRIBLE** gurnip that even the bravest ogres wouldn't mess with! A royal rumpscallion! A bloodthirsty bully, infamous for sentencing the cruellest and most GUT-SKUDDLING punishments on anyone who got on her nerves or didn't obey her every wish.

Right at that moment I knew two things for sure. Firstly, I'd massively underestimated Grogbah and his tricksy ways, and secondly … **I WAS DOOMED!**

The goblin officers and their captain led me along the jetty in the direction of the beach, and for a second I thought we were going back to dry land. No such luck.

We reached a point where the street on the promenade above juts out to sea alongside the pier and I was quickly pulled over to a big circular sewer grate that trickled dirty water and smelled like Granny Regurgita after she's eaten too much cabbage and bungbean stew.

There was a jangle of keys – I remember that bit – and right before Captain Grumpwhistle yanked the grate open on its ancient hinges and bundled me inside, I … well … I know this might seem a bit smooshy and dribble-wordy, but I turned and gasped when I saw **The Nothing To See Here Hotel.** My brilliant home. I'd almost never seen it from the outside at night … at least not from the gloomy shadows under the pier … and I hadn't realised how honkingly beautiful it was before.

Completely invisible to human eyes, it was dazzling to mine. The domes and turrets were gleaming in the stormy sky, and thousands upon thousands of windows twinkled like the lights on a Drooltide tree.

Behind those windows, I knew our guests would be getting ready for bed, nattering in the garden, drinking bluebottle brandy on the observatorium veranda, or just curling up with their loved ones – and that's when I thought of mine.

Everyone I knew. Mum, Dad, Nancy, Maudlin, Ooof, Granny … Everyone who could save me was inside the hotel, and none of them had a clue where I'd gone.

I glanced up and saw the lights were still on in Granny Regurgita's tower-bedroom at the top of the building, and then … it was over. My family and friends, my pet pygmy soot-dragon and my life at the hotel vanished as I was carried into the sewers and the iron grate swung closed behind us with a huge and echoey

CLAAAAAANNNGGG–ANG–ANG!

INTO THE DARK AND DOOKY DEEP

It was pretty clear straight away that we hadn't entered just any old human sewer tunnel.

Don't get me wrong ... I haven't exactly spent much time in them, but unless I'm seriously mistaken, sewer systems don't have little lanterns in the shape of grinning goblin faces on the walls, and a royal canoe with gold-and-green seats docked in the sludgy foul-smelling stream of water.

'Get in,' Grumpwhistle grunted. He'd been wearing a face like a smacked bottom ever since I told him I didn't know who he was, and now in the flickering glow of the burning lamps, he looked meaner and more dangerous than ever. **'Now!'**

'Yes! Hurry up, Banistump,' said Grogbah as he floated over to the front of the narrow boat and kneeled on the edge. 'It'll be honkhumptious to see what Moomsie has in store after she lays her eyes on the revolterous human who snuffled her magnificent son. She'll be angrier than a lava-imp in a rainstorm and I'll be right by her side when she has you squished, you murderling.'

'You're lying, GROGBOG!' I barked at the little goblin prince, trying my hardest not to burst into tears. 'You were stupid enough to step on a sleeping fly-trap's tongue! I had nothing to do with it!'

'Oh, shut your mumble-hole,' Flott groaned, barging me into the canoe. I stumbled down and toppled onto the nearest seat, nearly falling straight over the edge and into … I don't want to think what was down there. 'All this gripin' in the pipin'! It's a wonder you haven't given us all nogginache.'

With that, Grumpwhistle and Lickspittle hopped in after us and we were off.

The goblin captain turned in his seat and jolted the spluttery motor to life with a hefty whack. It was older-looking than the yell-a-phone and steamed and hissed like a kettle as we started chugging along through the tunnels.

'I can't wait to park my peepers on the goblin city again,' Grogbah tittered at me as we left the mooring behind us. 'After all this time stuck haunting a squivelling snotling like you, and never being able to get too far from that rotsy hotel, I finally realised that if I want to travel as far away as my squibbly hometown, I've got to bring you with me. I'm a genius!'

Nobody replied.

'I bet I'll get a hero's whoppsy welcome!'

After a little way, the lanterns along the sewer walls ended and we passed into a cold and dismal gloom, followed by total dreadful darkness.

Now, if you've read any of my books before, you know that Frankie Banister would never let you get bored with all the details of a canoe ride that went on **FOR EVER** in the dark! I'm not even joking! The canoe juddered along for such a long time that

after a while I actually stopped silently sniffling about my family and started wondering if this was the terrible fate I was going to be punished with.

I know I'm one-quarter troll and can see like it's daytime in this kind of dooksy place, but there was nothing to look at anyway. Yep! If there's one thing I learned on that terrible night, it's that if you've seen one sewer, you've seen them all … especially when you travel for what seems like a stinky eternity.

At one point, it got so dull that Lickspittle serenaded us with a rendition of the goblin classic song, 'Who Left That in Grandma's Hat?'

Just when, out of pure brain-bungling boredom, I was starting to think that meeting Queen Latrina would actually be wonderful … things changed.

To begin with, it was only that the tunnels started sloping downwards and the flow of water was getting faster, but then strange, illuminated shapes began to appear out of the gloom ahead of us – and, was it me, or could I hear a distant rumble echoing up the pipes?

As we approached the glowing shapes, I saw that

they were in fact ENORMOUS mushrooms, growing through the brickwork on either side of the water. First one, then ten, then hundreds! I'd never seen anything like it. The bulbous things were bigger than the sun umbrellas around the swimming pool back at home, and shone in ghostly oranges and pale blues above our heads.

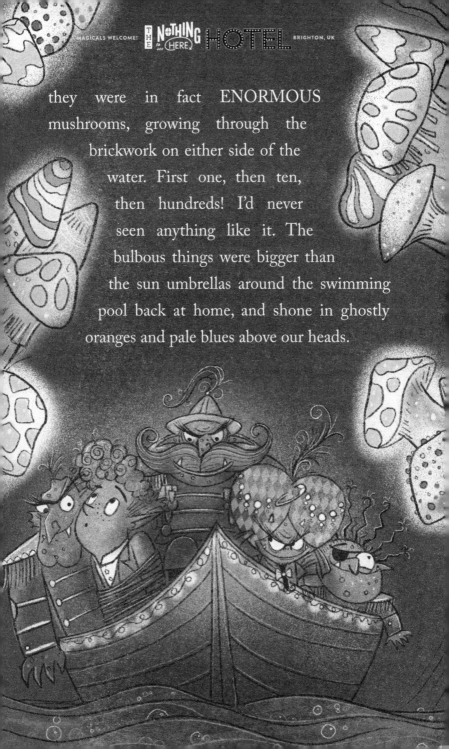

I remember thinking that Mr Croakum, the hotel gardener, would have cried with excitement at these bizarre growths, but at that time I had no idea how much more bizarre my night was going to get.

Before long, the distant rumble became a not-so-distant clamour, and our chugging canoe was whizzing through the toadstools at a tremendous speed.

'Woohoo!' Grogbah cooed from the pointed bow of the boat. **'I love this part! We must be near!'** He reminded me of Viscera Von Tangle, holding on for dear life at the front of the food trolley, and I felt another pang of sadness.

Not for long, though …

The narrow sewers widened as we sailed into an entire forest of mushrooms. Almost immediately I started spotting magical creatures, like fungus fairies and poison-punks, whizzing between the massive plants' stalks. We nearly crashed into a nokken (a Norwegian water troll) as it surfaced right in front of us, and a family of pond-gorpers had to dive to safety when our canoe splashed through their laundry pool.

And then?

WHOOOOOOOOOOOOOOMFFF!

WELCOME TO GRADIBASH

The giant mushrooms had been so dense and thick, I hadn't noticed the open mouth of a sluice-gate rushing up towards us. There was a great surge of water and a tremendous splash as we rocketed out of the gloom and into a light that was so blinding, I nearly toppled backwards off my seat in the canoe.

'Ha! I did that the first time,' Flott laughed, grabbing me by the shoulder and steadying me. 'Only takes a weensy second for your eyes to adjust.'

I squinted and tried to see through the rainbow-glare that hit us, then nearly fainted when our surroundings came twinkling into view. It was a scene I'd looked at loads of times in my great-great-great-grandad's old black-and-white photo albums.

There was no mistaking it – we'd just arrived in

Gradibash; city of the Barrow Goblins.

'Here we are,' Captain Grumpwhistle said, slowing down the frantically puttering engine.

'We're here!' Grogbah yelled in his annoying little voice, and started fussing with his phantom clothes, making sure there weren't any wrinkles. **'Wee!'**

'Good,' Lickspittle joined in. 'I'm starvatious. Let's head into the warrens and get some noshlies.'

I swear to you, my reader friend, every impressive thing I'd ever seen before that moment suddenly became boring and ugly. I couldn't believe my peepers! It was exactly like the copy of the map I'd seen visiting Abe's office down in the Briny Ballroom.

We'd emerged into the Great Cistern Lake at the centre of the city and – well – the Dark and Dooky Deep wasn't dark and dooky at all!

All around us, the limitless buildings rose up the walls of the cavernous cistern like tea leaves clinging to the inside of a giant teacup, and everything was illuminated.

'What did I tell you?' Grogbah suddenly squealed.

We all jumped and stared at the little ghost, hopping from curly-toed shoe to curly-toed shoe. 'My hero's welcome! They've come to greet me!'

Grogbah pointed to something behind us and we turned, startled to find the excited faces of thousands upon thousands of goblins staring in our direction.

'Oh, blunkers!' Grumpwhistle mumbled to himself. 'I wasn't expecting that!'

They were everywhere! The dockside was so jam-packed with jostling goblins, it looked like any second now they were all going to start plopping off the edge into the water. There were crowds on the bridges and packs of whooping underlings on every balcony I could spot, and all of them were waving flags and banners that said ... that said ...

'WELCOME, DEADLING!' Grogbah read out loud. 'That's me!' He turned to Captain Grumpwhistle and started flapping his arms like an agitated rooster. 'Quick, Pugnacious, take us over to the marina. I want to meet my adoring subjects.'

Grumpwhistle groaned under his breath and steered us towards the thronging docks.

The hordes of excited goblins started cheering louder and louder as we approached, until their voices were echoing all across the city.

'My people and peoplets!' Grogbah sobbed. 'Be still, my clunkered heart!'

By the time Flott and Lickspittle had tied the boat up to the quayside and we'd climbed the stone steps onto the dock, Grogbah had already flown ahead and was curtsying like a broken jack-in-a-box.

'It's true, I have returned!'

There was an odd moment of sudden silence as the crowds drew in a sharp breath and the five of us stared back at them in their hundreds, not quite knowing what to do. After a minute of nudging and pushing, a thin smartly dressed goblin with a bald patch on the top of his head stepped towards us.

'Umm ...' He looked more nervous than I felt. 'Umm ...'

I spotted a little badge on his lapel with the same symbol as the desk-sign in Bambus Boatswig's office.

M-T-T-T?

What was it again? Something about magical tourists, travellers and ... I couldn't remember the rest.

'M-m-m-my name is Grub,' the scrawny goblin stammered. 'Grub Crackshins.'

'Don't be shy, good peasant!' Grogbah beamed, taking another bow and a few curtsies.

'My name is Grub Crackshins, and on behalf of the city of Gradibash, I'd like to welcome you and hope you have a plunkly stay.'

The mass of excited goblins hollered and shouted and waved their banners.

'Oh, you're too kind,' Grogbah simpered. He opened his wonky mouth to speak again, when the little travel-goblin called Grub turned to him and …

'I'm terribly sorry,' he said to the ghostly prince. 'Would you mind keeping it down for a minute? I'm trying to welcome the deadling and you're ruining it a little bit.'

· 12 ·

THE DEADLING

Grogbah looked like he'd been smacked around the chops with a wet kipper.

'WHA—' he blurted. 'But I'm Prince Gro—'

'Shhhh!' an elderly goblin-granny hissed. 'Skuddle off, will you?'

The little ghost wailed like a banshee who'd missed breakfast and threw himself at a pile of crates and old ropes.

'We don't normally do all this for deadlings,' Grub said after a pause. He turned his attention to me. 'But we've never had a human visit the city before, and we thought it would be a blunkin' shame if we didn't show you a beamly nice time before Queen Latrina has you …' He mimed squashing something in his hands, then grinned at me like it was the best news in the world.

I WAS THE DEADLING! I clenched my bottom and felt my knees start to shake.

In the darkness of the canoe ride I'd been secretly praying that Grogbah was lying as usual. He **NEVER** tells the truth about anything. But everything he'd said was real! I'd actually been brought all this way just to be scrumpled by his murderous mother!

'Skudderous revenge doesn't have to be entirely awful,' Grub continued with a sweet smile as he spotted the fear on my face. 'Shall we?'

With that, the little goblin turned and beckoned us to follow. I tried to struggle against Officer Flott's trap-lace but it was pretty clear that wasn't going to do any good.

Grumpwhistle placed a hefty hand on my shoulder then turned to Grogbah. The grizzling ghost was now sitting on a barrel, sulking and sighing.

'Are you coming, Your Princeliness?'

'No!' Grogbah stropped with a grimace. He scooted around on his bottom, facing away from us. 'This should be my welcoming party! Tell Moomsie I'm staying here and I'm not moving until I get my own parade to the palace!'

'Suit yourself,' Grumpwhistle muttered. 'Let's be off.'

He turned back round, nodded to Grub and I was led away from the docks towards my fate.

'TAKE HIM TO THE PALACE!'

'To your left you'll see the Great Gradibashi Opera House,' Grub indicated, as curious goblins ran along on both sides of the pavement to get a better look at the human child being paraded through the streets, 'And that's the monument to King Halitosis the Third over on your right.'

'Boring,' Lickspittle moaned to herself, thinking no one would hear.

I don't know what I expected Gradibash to be like – well, actually I do, and it was nothing like this. The city was built centuries ago in the deepest sewers, so I thought it would be more like Granny Regurgita's hometown.

Granny took me there to visit once and it was a right muckdump, let me tell you. Even she said so!

The town of Underneath where Granny Regurgita was born and raised was all rickety huts and putrid alleyways filled with troll-bandits and fighty-types, but not here – not even close.

With every turn we made on the wide thoroughfares we passed vast music-halls, and art galleries and noisy casinos. We marched along Snootle Boulevard and Prawk Prong Street, then turned right onto Hungdunkem Avenue. There were entire arcades of fancy-looking fashion stores, where goblins were coming and going with armfuls of expensive shopping bags, wearing the craziest clothes and swankiest hats I'd ever seen.

'And round this bend is the Just-About-In-The-Middle Bridge,' Grub announced as we turned a corner under one of the giant glowing mushrooms. They were just like street lamps in Gradibash. 'Across the water, on the other bank of the Great Cistern Lake, you'll see …'

A gurgly cocktail of fear and amazement rushed

through me for the squillionth time that night as I beheld Queen Latrina's palace.

The building was so grand it made **The Nothing To See Here Hotel** look like Mr Croakum's garden shed! I gawped in wonder as I realised that every bit of it – every wall and roof and door and buttress, and all the other parts I didn't know the names of – was made from COLOURED GLASS!

It was incredible. The entire palace was like one gargantuan stained-glass window and it was more beautiful than anything I'd ever seen.

'Isn't it dazzly?' Grub asked with a sigh.

I nodded, but I wasn't exactly feeling in the right mood for sightseeing, and as we made our way across the bridge, I could only repeat the same words to myself again and again in my head:

'Grogbah's mum lives in there, Frankie Banister, and she's going to squish you!'

THE COURT OF QUEEN LATRINA

'I'm afraid this is as far as we're allowed to go,' said Grub as we reached the gargantuan green-glass doors of the palace, covered from top to bottom in intricate swirls of goblin runes.

'What?' I asked. 'Why's that?' So far, Grub was the only friendly Barrow Goblin I'd met and I suddenly wished he could stay with me.

'Because, to the queen, we're scumlies and street-rottlers. Us poor pluglets who live outside the palace are forbidden from ever entering.' Grub sighed and gave a nervous smile. 'She says we give her the squitlies.'

'Quite right,' Flott butted in, then shrugged and pulled on a bell handle mounted to the purple-glass wall. 'Better to be safe than squitly.

That's what my grandpops used to say.'

'Very wise,' Lickspittle joined in.

There was a loud **DONG** from somewhere inside, and in no time at all, I could make out the shapes of goblin-servants running about on the other side of the glass. They pressed their faces against it, peering out at us. And when they saw that the captain's latest prisoner had arrived, the towering green doors glided silently open.

'I hope you enjoyed the tour,' Grub said, giving a little bow. 'And I hope you don't get too … umm … dead.'

'Follow me, Banister boy,' Captain Grumpwhistle grunted as he strode inside. It was obvious he'd been to the palace loads of times before, and Lickspittle, Flott and I had trouble keeping up as we crossed an ornate entrance hall with lines of goblins standing all the way along the walls.

'Are those servants?' I whispered to Lickspittle.

'Yep,' she whispered back, enjoying the excursion. 'Posher than a poutypooper's purse.'

I couldn't believe it when I saw the rows of

handmaidens, attendants, footgoblins and guards, all wearing the finest silks and pearls and neck-ruffs. These were Queen Latrina's waiting-staff and they were dressed in even better fashion than the goblins I saw shopping in the city!

'I like this next room, I do,' Flott announced to us both, with a wicked glint in his eye. 'It's proper good.'

'What's in there?' I asked.

'Just you wait.' Flott nodded as the next set of doors swung open and we passed into a long corridor of blue glass that was lined with painting, after painting, after painting.

Every golden frame was filled with the miserable

portrait of a grim-looking goblin nobleman, with their names engraved below in loopy writing.

Lord Putrus of the frump forests ... Admiral Mungit Storm-strider ... Duke Dinglethwait VIII ... Baron Umpus Oglington-Smulch ...

'Who are these gonkers?' I whispered. Something about the paintings' unhappy expressions filled me with dread. 'They all look so grizzly.'

'This is the Hallway of Husbands,' Lickspittle giggled. 'Bleuurgh!'

'The queen has this many husbands?' I gasped.

'*Had*,' Flott replied. 'The queen *HAD* this many husbands. They don't last long around here.'

Oh, blunkers! She's even worse than I already thought!

We reached the end of the hallway, where Captain Grumpwhistle was waiting impatiently for us before another door – turquoise this time.

'Now, boy,' he growled, leaning so close I could smell his sour breath and feel his twizzly moustache tickling my nose. 'There'll be no funny business or tomfoobling on my watch. Is that clear?'

I nodded silently, trying to ignore the pain in my ribs. It felt like something was actually poking me repeatedly, but I didn't have time to think about it now.

'No snizling! No running! No rudey-roaring! You're about to meet the Ruler of the Dark and Dooky Deep, and I'll be a mumple's munkle if I let you be disrespectabus on my watch. GOT IT?'

I nodded again, giving serious thought to collapsing on the shimmering floor and playing dead.

'Righty, then.' Grumpwhistle suddenly beamed with a false grin, then spun on his heels and flung the doors behind him wide open. 'In we go!'

I couldn't see round the captain's melon-head and wide, sloping shoulders, but there was an audible gasp from inside the next chamber and the sound of enthusiastic chattering.

'Hold your hooters!' Grumpwhistle yelled into the room. 'I present my new prisoner!'

Cries of alarm rang out, and I could hear high-pitched yelping as Grumpwhistle marched ahead with Flott and Lickspittle pulling me along behind them.

As we passed under the high archway, I caught sight of the owners of the wailing voices. I was being led down the centre of a huge open courtyard, crammed full of courtiers who looked more like Drooltide decorations than stumpy magical creatures, and they were all holding their noses.

'Ugh! It's common and disgusterous!' A nearby goblin-maiden retched. **'IT STINKS!'**

'Make it go away!' screamed an old goblin lord in a wheelchair, with a beard so long it trailed along the floor and tangled in the wheel-spokes. 'It looks angry! Does it bite?'

'Where are its warts?!' a particularly knobbly

goblin lady with a face like a dropped omelette yowled. I couldn't help but scowl back at her as she waggled her stump of a finger at me. 'It's the ugliest thing I've ever seen in my life!'

'**Calm yourself, lords, ladies, and lumplies! Fear not!**' the captain called over the assembly. He flourished his cape and puffed out his round chest. 'As you can see, my elite officers have this mad-eyed murderling under control.'

Lickspittle grinned and waved at everyone in the room, dropped her end of the golden rope, then quickly fumbled to pick it up again.

Captain Grumpwhistle rolled his eyes and shook his head for the tiniest of seconds. 'As I was saying,' he growled through gritted teeth, 'you are quite safe from this vicious beast while I'm here to protect you.'

'Bring it before the queen!' a jester in a jangly hat cried. 'She'll want to know it's arrived!'

'Yes!' the courtiers joined in. 'Alert the queen! She'll deal with it perfectly!'

'EXCUSE ME!' a piggy-nosed goblin in gold silk gasped. 'I'm the royal advisor! I think I'll decide when we alert the queen!'

'Very well,' Grumpwhistle said, folding his arms and tapping a foot. 'You decide …'

The royal advisor paused for a moment, until …

'ALERT THE QUEEN!' he shouted before gesturing dramatically to the far end of the open plaza. The crowd hurriedly parted and I braced myself to see Grogbah's grotesque mother for the first time. I turned with my eyes slightly closed in case the sight was truly dreadful, but …

Oh …

The far end of the courtyard, where I guessed the queen should be, was completely empty. There wasn't even a throne! The only sign that something should be there was a raised stage with three little steps leading up to it and an ornately embroidered curtain hanging behind it, concealing some other part of the palace.

'Where is she?' I said out loud. The lumpish goblin woman heard me and cackled.

'Errgh! It's brainless too!' she balked. 'Doesn't it know the queen never enters a room without a jazzly fanfare?'

'It's noggin-bonked!' yelled another. 'They probably don't even have brains where it comes from!'

'Or fanfares!' laughed Omelette Face.

As if on cue, a quartet of goblin musicians struck up a regal blast of music and I watched as the curtain behind the stage parted.

Now, this is one of those moments when I have to promise you I'm telling the truth …

From behind the peacock-coloured drapes stalked a monstrous crocodile! **HONESTLY!!!!**

HERE SHE IS!

The creature was ten times bigger than I was, brandishing teeth as fearsome as any nifflehog or Madagascan muskrumple, and plate-sized scales of every colour from green to brown to black. The colossal reptile prowled out onto the raised platform as all the goblins (including Grumpwhistle, Flott and Lickspittle) bowed and curtsied.

'Your Greatness!'

'Long live Her Majesty!'

'We are your humble servants!'

I didn't know whether to faint or laugh or scream! All this time whingy-whiney Grogbah had been the son of … a crocodile!

'Welcome!' howled the royal advisor. 'Queen Latrina!'

Just then, as the terrifying animal lugged more of its terrible torso onto the stage, I caught sight of something I would never have guessed at, even if you gave me ten billion tries and tons of clues. It looked like I might have got slightly carried away, thinking the queen was a big spiny monster.

As the creature clomped into the courtyard, a squat golden throne appeared, strapped to the crocodile's back and round its belly, as if it was wearing a rucksack. The tiny chair emerged from behind the curtain and sitting in it was what I can only describe as a crazy-eyed pumpkin in a party frock.

'Steady there, Doris!' the little goblin commanded, blinking through enormous riding goggles. She had a set of reins clutched in her stubby hands that stretched out to a metal ring in the crocodile's nostrils. 'Whoa, girl! Left a bit!'

The gathering of courtiers bowed and curtsied even lower.

'How's that for an entrance, you great big bunch of skuzzlers?' the queen guffawed at the room of goblins. 'Make way, peasants!'

There was another long moment of excited chattering as we all beheld Latrina, Queen of Gradibash.

I had to muster every bit of strength I could not to laugh. As scared as I was, Latrina looked like something you'd see in a demented toyshop. She couldn't have been much taller than my knee when she was standing on the ground and her silver dress was so floofed with layers, it looked like she should be attached to the end of a very expensive mop! Also ... I could see where Prince Grogbah got his looks from. They certainly ran in the family.

'Where are my snacklies and tasty treats?' Latrina hollered as a team of goblin servants busied themselves with trays of delicate cakes and tarts. 'Strike up the band! Shower me with gifts! Someone fetch my croco-steps!'

Pandemonium broke loose as the queen yanked on the crocodile's reins again and the spiny creature thudded round in a full circle, swatting the quartet of musicians halfway across the floor with its tail.

'Reversing!' Latrina screamed. 'Reversing! No! This way, Doris!'

The confused crocodile started clomping around in the other direction and one of the poor servants was batted straight over the nearest wall, tray of treats and all.

'You're not listening, Doris. I'm in charge! **I'M IN CHARGE!'** Latrina threw herself forward and back in her throne like a child having a tantrum when their ride is over on the amusements at Brighton Pier. **'DOWN, GIRL! DOWN!'**

Finally, with the queen yanking the reins left and right, the crocodile backed over to the side of the raised stage and settled onto its scaly belly.

'That's better,' Latrina cooed. 'Who's a good girl?' She took a moment to straighten her goggles and the little crown that had slipped over to one side of her knobbly head, then turned in her golden chair and looked down at her royal subjects for the first time. 'Greetings, you rancid rottlers!'

'Greetings, Your Majesty!' the courtyard of goblins echoed in unison. 'You are looking more beauty-tootiful than ever!'

'Mmmmm …' the queen grunted in agreement as she poked her little finger in her ear, wiggled it about, then pulled it out and examined how much wax was stuck to it. 'I know!'

'Seeing you has brightened our lives even more than yesterday,' the crowd cooed together. Something told me this was very well rehearsed.

'I should blunking think so,' Latrina replied. **'WHERE ARE MY CROCO-STEPS?'**

Two servants hurried over to the side of the queen's crocodile with a little set of golden steps. They placed them just below where the throne was buckled round its middle, then set about helping Latrina down from her perch.

'You, take my hand,' she barked at one of them, before turning to the other. 'And, *you*, support the royal rump!'

After lots of shoving and grabbing and several flashes of the royal panty-bloomers, the pumpkin-sized ruler was hauled down to the stage and she stomped forward, eyeing the gathered courtiers in the same way my dad eyes the kitchen sink when it's his turn to do the washing-up.

'Let's get this honkswizzle over and done with,' she moaned, grabbing a slice of mustard and mouse gristle tart from the nearest tray, sniffing it and then throwing it on the floor. 'Euuurgh!'

Captain Grumpwhistle raised his hand and opened his mouth to address the courtyard, when …

'Ummm … If I may speak first, Your Greatness?' The royal advisor in his fancy cloak and feathered hat stepped forward again.

'Who are you?' the queen snapped. 'You're ugly!'

'I'm the royal advisor, Your Majesty.'

Latrina pulled a face.

'We talk every day … about very important things,' the royal advisor said with a nervous smile. 'Remember? I have lots of matters to discu—'

'Well, I can't be expected to memorise every last one of you dungles!' the queen shrieked. 'Disgusterous grublings all look the same to me. You all look like a boggart's back-bits!'

The entire room tittered and fanned themselves with coy smiles on their faces.

'Indeed. Thank you, my queen. You are kind as ever,' the royal advisor simpered. 'So ... may I continue?'

Latrina grunted again. She lifted her riding goggles up onto her blotchy forehead and sneered when she got a better view of everyone.

'FINE! Just get on with it. I'm having my verrucas shaved in the Royal Bubble-arium in a bit, and Doris is getting her claws painted. Very important stuff!'

'Y-yes, Your Majesty,' the nervous goblin continued. 'Here are today's announcements!'

As I watched all this unfold, a tiny sense of relief crept into my brain. Maybe Grogbah hadn't been completely truthful after all – that little fibbler. Queen Latrina clearly wasn't too keen to have a chat with me, like he'd said, and it seemed like she wasn't expecting my arrival at all. I was also super pleased to be right at the back of the courtyard and had managed to half-conceal myself behind a huge fern in a pot as big as a bathtub. With any luck, Latrina wouldn't even spot me.

'*Ahem.*' The royal advisor unravelled a long scroll and started reading from it. 'Many of the palace servants are hungry and starvatious …'

'The moany-mopers! If they're nibblish it means they're still alive! They should count themselves very lucky indeedy!' Latrina replied. 'Plus nail-biting and nose picky-licking is always very nutritious. They can eat as much of that as they like.'

'**YOUR MAJESTY IS WHOPPSY WISE!**' the courtiers chirped together.

'The royal guards caught a cruminal stealing frog grog from the Royal Kitchens,' the advisor-goblin read.

'Flush them down the poodly-pipe!' Latrina ordered. By now she was shovelling snacks from several food platters into her mouth and spat pie crust all over the royal advisor's cape as she spoke.

'The crown prince of the compost pooks arrived three weeks ago and has been waiting for you in the palace hedge maze ever since, Your Majesty,' the royal advisor read from the list, not daring to brush himself down from all the bits of chewed food. 'He's visiting from Kew Gardens and is another contender for your next husband, the lucky thing. Would you like to meet with him?'

Queen Latrina contorted her face like she was going to be sick.

'Flush him down the poodly-pipe as well!' she hollered.

'Righty … Erm …' The royal advisor was looking more and more flustered by the second. 'Well, there's the small matter of invading armies of thistlewumps from the south-west sewers. Any thoughts?'

'Don't care!' Latrina bawled.

'The autumn sea-kelp harvest is nearly upon us …'

The queen fake-yawned loudly.

'You've received a very special gift from the Mayor of the Underneath in return for a spot of junkumfruit trading.'

'Oh, what is it?' Latrina's eyes flashed greedily. 'Tell me, tell me, tell me!'

'Five hundred bouquets of finkus flowers.'

Latrina looked completely insulted and wrinkled up her pudgy nose.

'Is that all?' she groaned. 'Weeds?'

'I'm afraid so, Your Majesty.'

'Flush them down the poodly-pipe!' the queen screamed so loudly, even Doris the crocodile flinched. 'D'you know what? I'm bored now. Everything else on that stupidly little list of yours …'

'Yes?' The royal advisor's face had turned as white as a little green goblin's face could possible go.

'Flush it all down the poodly-pipe! All of it! **EVERY LAST THING! WHOOSH!'**

THERE SHE GOES!

It was gobsmacking to see Queen Latrina holding court. She was even more bonkers than Grogbah! If I hadn't been worrying about what the beach-ball-in-a-ball-gown might do to me, I'd almost say it was fun to watch.

At that moment, however, Lickspittle waved in the air and yelled,

'WHAT ABOUT THE BANISTER BOY?'

Everyone in the royal plaza fell silent for a moment and turned to look in my direction.

'Oh, good gracicles!' the omelette-faced goblin gasped, clutching at her hundreds of pearls. 'I clean forgot old stinky-poos over here!'

'We can't miss the human out!' croaked the ancient goblin in the wheelchair. 'I want to see a public scrounching!'

'Ooh-ho-ho! You're in for it now, whelpling,' Flott chuckled next to me, rubbing his hands together. 'I love a good spot of revenging before supper.'

Queen Latrina, who had been busy snatching drinks from a nearby servant and guzzling them down with little volcanic burps, stopped in her tracks and placed her tiny fists on her hips.

'What's going on?' she snapped. **'Why isn't your attention all on me?'**

Before anyone else could speak, Captain Grumpwhistle stepped out with a flamboyant swish of his blood-red cape, and the goblin courtiers cleared aside.

'Your Majesty,' he declared. 'I have returned from the Great Outside with your precious cargo!'

'Oooh, Grumpkins!' the queen chortled, clapping her hands. 'It's you! Back from where? What have you brought me?'

I watched with a pounding heart as the captain swaggered into the centre of the court. This was it. My time had run out. A cold tingle of despair crept up my spine.

'I battled through mushroom forests!' Grumpwhistle boomed.

'**Oooooh,**' the crowd replied.

'Ventured to gut-rotsy goblin fishing towns and the human city of Brighton!'

'**HONKHUMPTIOUS!**' Queen Latrina squawked.

'My courageous officers, Flott and Lickspittle, walked amongst **PEOPLE** under the disguise of a glimmer!'

'Overlings? Cor! Is it true humans all have honking great fat and heavy feet?' one of the courtiers asked with wide eyes. 'So they don't get blown away by the wind up there?'

'YES!' Lickspittle butted in. 'I saw it with my own peepers!'

'Squibbly stuff!' Latrina said with a grin spreading across her green and lumpy face. 'So …

don't keep me waiting or I'll get crossly. What did you bring me?'

'What you asked for, Your Majesty,' Grumpwhistle said with a low bow. 'The very thing you demanded I collect.'

'I don't remember demanding you to collect anything!'

'It's just what you wanted.'

'So, show me!' the queen grunted.

'Your Majesty will be so pleased.' Grumpwhistle beamed. 'You will be so happ—'

The stumpy queen said nothing for a second, and then her face twisted into a scowl that could have smashed windows, it was so hideous.

'JUST TELL ME, GRUMPKINS! I DON'T LIKE WAITING!' she bellowed. **'I'M TOO BUSY RULING THIS BUNCH OF SNIPE-SNIFFERS TO REMEMBER EVERYTHING I DEMAND!'**

Even a brute like Grumpwhistle knew not to mess with the hopping-mad little Brussels sprout.

He turned round and gestured for Flott and Lickspittle to bring me forward.

By this point I'd hidden myself as far behind the giant fern as I possibly could, but no sooner had I pulled against the two officers, the trap-lace tightened round my middle and I had to give up.

I was yanked into the clearing of goblins at the centre of the plaza and an audible gasp went up around the place.

Latrina stared blankly at me, like she had no clue what she was even looking at.

'I bring you Frankie from **The Nothing To See Here Hotel**,' the captain cheered. He flourished his arms at me as if he'd just performed a magic trick.

'A Frankie … what?' the queen finally asked. She looked more baffled than a hippopotamus on a helter-skelter.

'Frankie Banister! The slayer of your sovereignly son,' Grumpwhistle tried again in an even more excited voice. 'A descendant of **ABRAHAM BANISTER!**'

'Abraham Banister?' Queen Latrina's eyes started widening. 'The pukey-pootling husband of that hulkus honker, Regurgita Glump?'

'The very same,' Grumpwhistle declared. 'And this is his great-great-great-grandson!'

'A … a … human?'

To say that Queen Latrina screamed loudly, would have been like saying that Gradibash was only a bit impressive. Yep! The gristly old grunion screeched such a high-pitched wobbler of a howl,

the front row of her audience fell backwards and slid across the glass mosaicked floor.

'A HUMAN!?' she bawled. 'You brought a grotsome, snivelling, stink-ball-on-legs **HUMAN** into my magnificent palace!? **It's filthous! It's hidyump! It's gruzzly!'**

'Your Majesty, you asked me to!' Grumpwhistle started flapping his hands at the hysterical queen like he was trying to put out a fire. 'You sent me orders. Remember?'

'I did no such thing!' Latrina squealed. 'Do you want me to get squitly right here in the Royal Throne Hall? **DO YOU!?!?'**

'You said you wanted to meet the boy because of—'

'TAKE IT AWAY!' the queen barked hysterically. 'Take this rot-riddled thing back to where it came from now, or I'll blurgle all over you! **I'LL BLURGLE ALL OVER EVERYONE!'**

With that, the furious little ruler of the **DARK AND DOOKY DEEP** turned and started scrambling back up the golden croco-steps to her fearsome throne.

REVENGE

For the first time since I'd wandered into the hotel library and the wonky glimmer of my mum had transformed into a pair of grizzly kidnappers, I felt the faintest spark of hope in my chest.

'Why would you bring it in here?!' Latrina hollered over her shoulder as she tried to heave herself up the side of her pet crocodile. **'BAD GRUMPWHISTLE! BAD!'**

Had it really all backfired? This quest for revenge had gone wrong, and Grogbah's bonkers mother didn't have the foggiest clue about why I was there. How could the captain have made such a mistake?

I looked at Grumpwhistle and his stupid sidekicks with a victorious smile and they glared back, fuming with rage.

'Well,' I said, feeling a bit too over-confident for my own good. I think I even laughed in the captain's face. 'It's about time you and your noggin-bonked officers took me back ...'

'MOOMSIE!!'

There was a small explosion of ectoplasm above the fussing crowd and – you guessed it – Grogbah appeared, looking more miserable than ever. His curly toed shoes had drooped into sad dangly rat-tails and there were slimy tears running down his ruddy cheeks.

'Moomsie, I'm not speaking to your botty-bot!' the prince whined. 'Turn round, please!'

'What the **BLUNKERS?** Doris, did you say something?' Queen Latrina was still struggling up onto her crocodile and the entire room watched as her stubby legs waggled about in our direction, sticking out of her pompom of petticoats.

She finally scrambled onto the gold throne, then jerked back around, looking dishevelled and confused.

'Who said that?'

'It was me, Moomsie-woo!' Grogbah did a quick spin in the air. 'Your speshly prince. Your smoochikins! Did you forget my parade?'

Latrina gawped at the ghost of her son. She opened up her mouth to speak, closed it, then opened it again.

'Oooooh, not you!' she finally snapped. 'I heard you'd kicked the carbuncle at that **Nothing To Something Something Hotel** ages ago. Who's been telling me fibblies?'

'Moomsie!?' Grogbah grovelled. 'Aren't you happy to see your lumpling?'

'Bleurgh!'

'Your prince!' Grogbah whined. 'Your son and heir to the golden throne.'

'Heir to the what?' Latrina balked. 'Not on your nelly, you ain't! I'm leaving Gradibash to Doris. She'll look lovely in a crown and a sparkly dress.'

The crowd all gasped at this news, and the royal advisor fainted onto a plush pink sofa.

'Of course I'm the heir!' Grogbah sobbed back. 'I might be a bit ghosty and whispish, but that doesn't mean I can't be kingly as well.'

'Oh, this is all I need,' groaned Latrina, snatching up Doris's reins. 'I've got a human-stinking-being honking up my throne hall, and now my cowardly conk of a deadish son has snizzled back into the palace, thinking he can run things around here!'

Grogbah twisted in the air and yelped at me.

'Why is Frankie still here? I thought you would have clunkered him by now,' he blubbed at his mother. **'And I'm not a cowardly-conk!'**

'Yes, you are,' Latrina chuckled. 'A big'un! You're dim-twitted too.'

Grogbah turned to the sea of upturned goblin faces crowding the plaza and grizzled.

'You all love the Prince of Gradibash, don't you?' he said, puffing out his chest and trying to flex his muscles. 'I'm big and smart and impressively.'

The courtiers mumbled under their breath and stared at their feet, shuffling about.

'Nah,' wheezed the ancient goblin through his tangled beard.

'I prefer the crocodile,' confessed another.

'I've had enough of all this glubbergrunting and chattywagging,' Queen Latrina grumbled. She lifted the reins and was about to steer Doris back out of the courtyard. 'Make sure you send that snivelsome human back to where he came from, Grumpwhistle!'

Grogbah gasped.

'No, Moomsie! Frankie can't go back!'

'Nonkumbumps!' the queen grumbled. 'He's disgusterous … and his face is dreaderously ugly. Why can't he go back to where he came from?'

'That's what I'm trying to tell you!' said Grogbah. 'I can prove I'm not dim-twitted. It was my squibbly idea to bring him here from **The Nothing To See Here Hotel** in the first place.'

'What?' Captain Grumpwhistle grunted. 'I thought it was the queen's idea!'

'Well, I might have been slightly fibblish,' Grogbah explained. 'But I had to! I was stuck at the hotel haunting Frankie and couldn't get any further than the end of the street before I was pinged straight back to his slumish bedroom. I needed to make it home to Gradibash for my revenge, and I realised he was going to have to come with me. So I tricked some brain-boggled triplet tooth fairies in **The Nothing To See Here Hotel** to write two letters for me. Told them I was coming up with bedtime stories, I did, and the idiumps believed me. Ha! One note contained Captain Grumpwhistle's orders and the other was for the city's Board of Travel Goblins, announcing my glorious arrival with my human-prisoner. Then I snuck them both into the saddlebag of a visiting postal-goblin and my humdifferous plan was complete. That way I knew I'd get my whoppsy hero's welcome, and Banistump would be brought to Moomsie who could help me splat him. It was my idea all along! I'm super smartly ... and one successful plan out of two isn't bad!'

'Oh, that is good!' Lickspittle said, her mouth full of termite tarts. She gave Grogbah a round of applause.

You little rottler!' I yelled at the floating prince, who grinned spitefully at me. I've always known that Grogbah was tricksy, but fooling the Molar Sisters into helping him out was unforgivable.

'Moomsie, this horribump human chased me into a guzzly plant's gob and it grunched me up! Now it's time for you to wreak revenge for me. Promise your snuggly son you'll do it ... pleeeeaaaase.'

Queen Latrina shrugged.

'Not in the mood – I'm feeling a bit snoozerous,' she yawned. Then she yanked on Doris's reins and they started clomping out of the hall. 'Send the human back.'

'NO!' whimpered Grogbah.

'Send him back!' Latrina barked over her shoulder. **'NOW!'**

There was a moment of silence as we watched the bonkers ruler leaving, until …

'HE SAID TERRIBLE THINGS ABOUT YOU TOO, MOOMSIE!'

Queen Latrina and her crocodile stopped in their tracks.

'Awful, judderish things,' Grogbah went on. 'Really spinejangling.'

'No, I didn't, Grogbah!' I shouted as Doris thudded back round the way she'd just gone. 'Your Majesty, it's not true.'

'What kind of things?' Latrina grunted, narrowing her eyes at me.

'Ummm … well … he said you were a … a … a slimy slumpus!'

Queen Latrina's face fell into a scowl.

'And he said you've got … frazzly hair, like a hinkapoot … and crunchous elbows … and your crocodile is just a big bloated newt!'

'EH?' Latrina hollered.

'He also said that … umm … Gradibash is a muckdump and … err … your palace was a bit on the small and snizzly side!'

The queen's cheeks puffed out and her nostrils flared like a charging tusk-billed plunktipuss.

'I'll grottle you,' she roared at me. 'No one says my palace is small and snizzly without seeing the inside of the poodly-pipe!'

'Feed him to Doris!' Flott guffawed.

'Throw him in the lake!' cried the royal advisor, who'd come back to his senses and was now watching the scene unfold with wide eyes.

'Prickle his bumly-bits with rattle-snitches!' the goblin maidens chorused.

'NO, NO, NO!' Grogbah whined over the hubbub. 'Moomsie, Frankie Banister needs a much worse punishment. He's the most rotten kind of gurnip!'

I was frozen to the spot. It felt like I'd been prattle-peaced again, and no matter how hard I tried, my mouth wouldn't make a sound. The only thing I could think of was how far away I was from Mum and Dad, and I'm not ashamed to admit that I started crying and sniffling with fear. I'm only a kid!

'I know exactly what to do with you, you stinkly cruminal!' Latrina growled. She tugged on Doris's reins and the two prowled towards me. I was trembling all over with terror as the massive reptile clomped so close, I could feel its breath on my face and hear a deep, low rumbling from its belly.

'What are you going to do, Your Majesty?' the royal advisor clucked.

'Yes, Moomsie?' Grogbah cooed with glee. 'What have you got planned?'

Queen Latrina drew herself up to the top of her pumpkin-sized height, checked to see if her elbows were indeed a bit cruncheous, then glared at me with a face like thunder.

'IT'S GRIMEGORN FOR YOU, GRUBLING!' she bellowed. 'THROW HIM IN THE CLUNK!'

A cheer of praise and merriment went up around the courtyard of goblins. I watched with watery eyes as they all celebrated and approved my fate, but noticed the only person who wasn't hooting and hollering was Grogbah. He was staring at me with a look of determination on his piggy face.

Floating down slowly, the ghost-prince placed a cold spookery hand on my shoulder and leaned in close.

'Got you,' he whispered.

NOTHING to see HERE

WELL, HOW ABOUT THAT?

So, here we are. We've made it to Chapter Eighteen and I bet you hadn't guessed any of this was coming my way. I know I certainly hadn't.

If you'd have told me, back when I was racing around the hotel hallways with Viscera Von Tangle on the old food trolley, that by the end of the night I'd be being dragged along by a whole squadron of royal goblin guards on my way to jail, I'd have said you've been drinking too much bluebottle brandy!

The gaggle of Latrina's soldiers lugged me out of the palace and headed for a steep narrow road that led high up the edge of the great cistern. I followed it with my eyes and spotted a huge building with soaring grey walls and not a window in sight. Where the royal palace was beautiful, this place looked about as welcoming as a hug from a great white shark.

'Ooh, the queen picked a good one,' Lickspittle snickered as she jumped and skipped about alongside the marching goblins. 'I think I'd rather be eaten by Doris than end up in Grimegorn!'

'S'right,' Flott replied. 'No one gets out of that place.'

We trudged closer and closer to the frightful-looking building, and the nearer we got, I could feel my last little grains of hope trickling away. I was about to be locked up for ever and ever, and I'd

never see my **BRILLIANT** home or my family again.

Forgive me while I have another little cry – oh, all right – a huge belly-bungling sob.

END OF THE LINE …

And that was that …

I don't really have much else to tell you, my reader friend.

It didn't take long for the goblin guards to carry me inside that scary and unfriendly place, march me along a maze of windowless corridors, and throw me into a cell … and … I've been here ever since.

I'm eighty-seven now, with wonky teeth like cobble stones and hair so long and white, I can use it as a blanket at bedtime.

Thanks for reading my story and hope you had fun.

Bye, then …

The End.

FOOLED YOU!!

Ha! You didn't actually think one of my stories would end so miserabump and glumly, did you? Of course it doesn't! I'd never let it get so boring.

We haven't even got to the exciting stuff yet, I promise. There's plenty more to read about.

Where were we?

CELLMATES

'EUUURGH!'

The goblin guards
walked me along a maze
of Grimegorn's windowless
corridors until we reached a
large metal grate in the floor.
Then, without so much as a last
word or a goodbye, the rottlers
lifted it and dropped me inside.

I braced myself for a painful
bump like the one I got after I
fell through Bambus Boatswig's
ceiling … But instead I landed
on something thick and soft
and hairy.

'OH, CRIPES!' A startled lady's voice spoke in the darkness. 'Not again.'

I felt a mammoth hand reach up and pat me gently, and then it scooped its fingers round my belly and lifted me into the gloomy air.

'I need to stop sitting under that blunking grate, so help me,' the voice continued.

My magical eyes began adjusting to the shadows, helped by small lanterns glowing on the walls, and I watched as shapes started to appear.

'Round we come …' The mammoth hand twisted me upright, and I saw I was being held by a colossal … ummm … *thing*.

'Are you all right there, friend?' she asked, her warm brown eyes blinking questioningly at me. 'That horrible queen's guards never give anyone any warning around here.'

Coming face to face with what seemed like a friendly creature, especially after she beamed a great big smile, I could have wet my pants with happiness and relief. But I didn't think she'd appreciate me widdling in her hand, so I smiled back instead.

'I think so,' I stammered. 'Did I land on your head?'

'Indeed you did,' the huge creature chuckled. 'And good luck too. We're a long way from the floor.'

I glanced down and saw that I was high up near the rafters of the pitch-dark cell. Whoever this hairy lady-creature was, her head was wedged right near the roof.

'I'm Mrs Morkie, darling,' she said. 'Biddy Morkie. You made me jump, so you did, but there's no harm done.'

She examined me, like she'd just picked up something interesting at a jumble sale.

'So, who do I have the pleasure of plucking off my bonce?'

'I'm Frankie Banister,' I said. 'From **The Nothing To See Here Hotel**.'

'Well, I never,' Mrs Morkie chuckled. 'My old dadsy stayed there once, years and yearlies ago. Showed me all the photographs, he did.'

'Really?' I gasped.

'Really!' Mrs Morkie replied. 'He was too big to fit in any of the rooms, so those nice owners … umm … Regurgita and Albert made him a comfy bed from over a hundred sofa cushions in the foyer. He took up the whole space. Haha!'

'They're my granny and grandad! I said, feeling so happy to be talking about home. 'It's actually Regurgita and *Abraham* …'

'Oh yes, that's right! My mistake.'

'And they're not quite my granny and grandad. They're my great-great-great-granny and -grandad.'

'Blow me over with a blurtle's blow-hole!' Mrs Morkie huffed. 'Has it been that long?'

I nodded.

'Well, it's very nice to meet you, Frankie Banister,' the hairy giantess said. 'Come in and have a cup of tea.'

'You have to stop offering everybody tea, Morkie!' Another voice came out of the darkness somewhere below us. 'We haven't even got a teapot! Or a stove!'

I jolted with surprise. The huge fluffly creature had made me feel so suddenly calm and relaxed, my heart almost leaped into my throat when a different voice yelled.

'Oh, you'd better meet …' Mrs Morkie lowered me down to the ground and as my troll-eyes adjusted further, I saw a young faun walking towards me from the shadows carrying a candle, his hooves clip-clicking on the stone floor as he walked.

'Hello.' The faun extended a free hand to shake mine. He couldn't have been much older than me. 'I'm Gullivantus,' he said. 'But everyone calls me Gully.'

'Frankie,' I said. 'Nice to meet you, Gully.'

'Nice to meet you too. It's been ages since anyone has been thrown into Grimegorn.' Gully smiled, twitching one eyebrow mischievously. 'Do you know any jokes?'

I shook my head. There was no way I could remember any jokes just now.

'Never mind,' Gully said, grinning. 'Maybe later. At least we'll have something new to talk about – other than tea.'

'Oh, I am sorry,' Mrs Morkie winced. 'It's a force of habit. You can't spend two thousand years making endless mugs of ragwort tea and then just forget about it. It's like an itch that needs scratching.'

The giant fur-ball towering up near the murky ceiling laughed a deep resounding laugh.

'Wow! You're two thousand years old?' I gasped.

'Who's counting?' the enormous fluffball chortled.

'You don't look a day over one thousand seven hundred!' Gully giggled. 'You're practically a spring chicken.'

I don't think I'd ever heard a nicer sound than friendly voices laughing at that moment.

'Mrs Morkie, if you don't mind me asking,' I said as politely as possible, 'what are you? I've got hundreds of magical nature books back at home, only I've never seen anything like you in any of them.'

'You wouldn't have, sweetheart,' Mrs Morkie answered. 'My kind went into hibernation yonks and yonkers ago. I'm a cuddlump. Back in the old times, when humans and magicals lived peacefully and everyone needed a bit of a hug and some comforting tea once in a while, whole villages would visit us and have picnics on our bellies. It was lovely. We were the dinner ladies of the Dark Ages.'

'The Dark Ages!? What were they like?' I couldn't

help myself. 'I read a book about them in our library.'

'It was pitch-black. You couldn't see a thing!' The cuddlump shrugged. 'Kept tripping over everything. Trees were a nightmare.'

I smiled and wanted to ask more, but a cold breeze suddenly ripped through the cell and I remembered where I was with a nervous jolt.

Turning to look around, I saw for the first time that our dark jail had three stone walls and then one made entirely from tall iron bars.

'Welcome to your new home,' said Gully, noticing me glancing about. 'It's not as bad as it first seems. The toadstools outside have shrivelled for the day, but they'll grow back by the morning. Then you'll get a much clearer view of the place.'

I walked up to the bars and peered through. Even my magical eyesight couldn't pierce the gloom beyond them.

'So, this is prison?' I sighed after a while.

'Prison!?' Mrs Morkie said.

'Not quite. Is that what they told you?' asked Gully.

'Well … Umm …' I racked my brains. 'They didn't tell me anything.'

'Oh, those blunking goblins,' Mrs Morkie snapped. She eyed me with a look of sympathy on her huge face. 'I think we should all just get some sleep, and everything will be a lot clearer when the mushrooms come up.'

I didn't like the sound of that, but the mention of sleep reminded me of how exhausted I was. Who knew how many hours had passed since being grabbed in the hotel library?

'D'you want to snuggle in?' Mrs Morkie asked sweetly. 'You must be chilled to the chungles.'

'Yes, please.' I took off my bell-hop jacket and folded it into a pillow, then curled up next to the cuddlump's warm and fluffy ankle and immediately fell asleezzzzzzzzzzzzzzzzzzzzzzzzzzzzzzzzzzzzzzzzzzzzzz …

RUDE AWAKENINGS

Something hard and slightly wet bounced off my head with a dull thud, waking me from the deepest sleep I think I'd ever had.

'Ow!' I yelped.

'Good morning, Frankie!' Mrs Morkie's voice beamed above me. 'Did you snooze well?'

'Yep!' I yawned. The prison cell was light again now, and I spotted a half-chewed apple core on the ground next to me. The cuddlump must have been eating her breakfast and accidentally dropped it on my head.

'I've just been chatting to your little friend here,' Mrs Morkie continued. 'You didn't tell me there were two of you last night.'

'Hmmm?' I shuffled to my feet, wondering if I'd

heard correctly in my dozy state. Then I looked up and …

'**VISCERA!?** What are you doing here!?'

There, sitting on a tuft of Mrs Morkie's knee-hair like it was a tiny bed, was Princess Von Tangle herself.

'What do you think I'm doing here, Banister boy?' she snapped. The tiny piskie looked furious.

'I don't know,' I mumbled, rubbing my eyes. Was I still asleep?

'I'll tell you,' she squeaked. 'I knew that thing wasn't your mumsy the second I peeked into the stupid blunking library.'

'Why didn't you warn me?' I blurted.

'**I DID!**' Viscera shrieked. 'I climbed straight up the back of your trousers and into your jacket pocket, and **I'M ROYALTY! IN A POCKET! WE DON'T DO THINGS LIKE THAT, YOU KNOW!** I was yelling as loudly as I could, but as soon as that thing prattle-peaced you, it got me too!'

I felt like my jaw was about to hit the floor.

'By the time we got our voices back, there was no use trying to holler over a squillion gabbling goblins. I've been jabbing you in the ribs for hours, but you've been ignoring me!'

'So, that's what was poking me!' I said. 'I had no idea!'

'Well, while you were being taken off for a jolly trolliday, I was practically squished, you brainless bungle!'

'I'm sorry, Viscera,' I said. 'I have been a bit preoccupied.'

'Then you folded your jacket up like a pillow and nearly flattened me into piskie-pancakes with your massive head!'

'Well.' Mrs Morkie chuckled awkwardly. 'We're all here now, and that's the main thing.'

Just then, Gully wandered over, scratching one of his horns.

'What's all the fuss?' he asked lazily. 'I thought I heard another ... OH!'

'This is Vis ... err ... Visca ... Vipsy ...' Mrs Morkie tried to say. 'Vizzy ... Victor?'

'I am Viscera Von Tangle of the Lower Lumplands. Princess of the Piskish, Sovereign of the Squatlings, and I am **NOT IN THE MOOD!**'

'Right!' Gully gulped nervously. 'The pleasure is all mine.'

'Princess Von Tangle lives in the kitchen cupboard at the hotel. It turns out she was in my pocket this whole time,' I explained to the faun as he eyed the little piskie the way someone would look at an unexploded bomb. 'Viscera tried to warn me and … I didn't pay attention.'

'Ah, that's not too great, is it?' Gully pulled a pained expression. 'Are you all right?'

'Can I get anyone a cup of tea?' Mrs Morkie cooed.

'JUST SHUT UP, ALL OF YOU!' Viscera practically spat the words out. 'A princess must always be composed and I need some breathing room!'

'Viscera,' I said, stepping a little closer. 'If it means anything, I'm really happy to see you – and glad you're here.'

'Well, I'm not!' she squeaked back. 'Me – in a goblin prison!'

It was at that moment another apple core hit me in the back of the head with a dull *THUMP!*

'OW!' I yelled again. 'Who keeps doing that?!'

'This might actually be perfect timing,' Gully said, taking me by the arm. He led me a little way off from Viscera and Mrs Morkie, then looked me square in the eyes. 'Do you remember I told you this place was not quite what you thought it was?'

'Yes,' I said, rubbing the throbbing bump on the top of my head.

'Well, now's a good time for you to find out where Queen Latrina sent you. The apple cores are a part of it, I'm afraid.'

Then, without saying another word, Gully grabbed me by the shoulders and turned me round to face the prison bars.

GRIMEGORN: HAPPIEST PLACE IN THE WORLDS

The first thing I saw as I blinked in the mushroom light was a large bunch of multi-coloured balloons bobbing past, and I knew in an instant I'd got this place very wrong.

I gawped at the scene before me and couldn't bring myself to believe what I was looking at.

Beyond the iron bars of our cell was a huge ornate garden within an immense circular wall. There were palm-like trees swaying among the towering mushrooms, fountains, little bridges crossing streams and amusement carts dotted about, selling ice creams and snacks.

Everywhere I looked, I could see goblins strolling around, clutching cameras and pouches stuffed full

of maps, and vouchers, and guidebooks. A stumpy goblin lady dressed in an explorer's outfit – like the one Grandad Abe wears – was walking nearby with a large gabbling group following behind her.

'Keep up, ladies and gentlejims,' she called to them, an unconvincing smile plastered across her face. 'We've got so much to see on our tour today. Who's a first-time visitor?'

Several goblins in the group put their hands up and whooped.

'Yeah!' The guide cheered like someone who'd just got socks for the seventh Drooltide in a row. 'I think we should start off at the predator pens for some GRRRRRRuesome creature-watching. It's feeding time at the nifflehog enclosure in a weensy while.'

I looked over my shoulder at Gully.

'These are tourists?' I said.

'Yep.'

'And … and …'

I tried to take more of it in. Around the outside walls were prison cells just like ours, one after another. And I could make out various magical creatures in each one, shuffling about or sitting in the corners.

'These aren't prison cells!' I gasped. 'They're cages!'

'Yep!' Gully joined me at the bars and looked out too.

As if to answer my next question, another goblin

in an explorer's uniform approached through the garden with his tour group.

'All righty, folklies!' He beamed so enthusiastically, I thought he might be unwell. '**WELCOME TO GRIMEGORN SAFARI PARK!** A few rules – you can't steal any of the creatures to take home with you. No swimming in the jellyquarium. And stay away from the bars – some of these gruzzlers bite!'

LIFE IN THE CLUNK

Ever since I was super little, I've never understood zoos. They're **SO** weird!

I remember Mum telling me about them once. Who'd want to go and look at a miserable animal crumped up in a cage when they could see them living in the wild, just like they should be?

It's bumboozling, if you ask me.

So, you can imagine how juddered I was to find out that Queen Latrina had her own magical menagerie – and I was the newest exhibit! That gruntled old skrunt really was bonkers!

By the time the toadstools outside had grown to their full height for the morning, Grimegorn was teeming with visitors.

Viscera was still too hopping mad to even look at

me and had taken to sulking inside one of the little lanterns on the wall. The piskie princess was furious enough when she thought we were in prison, but when Gully broke the news that we'd ended up in a goblin zoo, she threw such a giant tantrum for a person no taller than my ankle, her paperclip crown glowed red with the heat.

'WHAT!?!' she screamed in her minute voice. 'Herded up like cud-chewing cattle!?'

'You're welcome to go, Princess,' I'd told her. 'You can easily walk straight through the bars, and I understand if you want to leave.'

'ME! Go out there amongst wildlings and weirdy-wumps? Not on your nelly, Banister boy! You got us into this mess and you will get us out of it!'

In the end, me and Gully decided to leave the tiny stropling alone for a while to cool off, so we went to sit near the bars and watched with fascination as families and gossipy groups made their way around the park.

'Is it like this every day?' I asked, gawping at a

new goblin who'd been posted outside our cage. He was dressed like … well … I think he was supposed to be dressed like a … a … human! He was wearing giant gloves and a big bulbous head made from stitched-together cloth. I could see his little face peering out through the thing's grinning mouth.

'Come and see Grimegorn's AMAZEROUS new addition!' he yelled as visitors hurried by. 'Feast your peepers on this, the most disgusterous and stinksome creature the worlds have ever seen!'

'It soon becomes quite normal.' Gully laughed. 'I think he's talking about you, by the way.'

I tried to laugh too, but I was feeling sick with sadness.

'We're going to grow old here, aren't we?' It felt like an enormous thump to my stomach.

'Try not to think about it,' Gully continued, putting his hand on my shoulder. 'It never helps.'

'It's all my fault,' I murmured, feeling tears welling up in my eyes.

'Do you know what they called me when I first

arrived, you disgusterous and stinksome creature?'
Gully joked, changing the subject.

I shrugged.

'They said I was a horned battle bungler.'

'How long have you been in here?' I asked, unable
to stop myself from chuckling.

'I don't really know,' Gully said. 'It's hard to keep
count of the days and nights when there's only
mushroom-light to go by. A long time, though.'

'Did you do something wrong?'

'Hmm?'

'I mean – ' I said, trying not to be rude – 'why
were you thrown in here?'

'Ah … that old story.' Gully groaned. 'Queen
Latrina decided she wanted a faun bodyguard. It
was fashionable at the time, or something – and
goblins love their fashion. She found out that the
troll mayor in the next town over had a team of faun
security guards and wanted one for herself.'

'That dreaderous queen!' Mrs Morkie scoffed,
from above. 'It makes my blood boil, it does.'

'Captain Grumpwhistle and his stupid officers

snitched me when I was asleep in the woods, but when they marched me all the way back to Gradibash, the queen was furious they'd only grabbed a little one. She got herself a giant crunkodile instead and I was thrown in this pla— OOOW!'

A half-eaten junkumfruit sailed into the cage and hit Gully square in the face with a loud **SQUELCH!** He toppled to the floor, covered in sticky slime.

'Make them do something, Moomsie!' a voice snivelled just outside the bars.

I turned to see a chubsome goblin child and his mother standing there, looking impatient. The squatling fixed his beady eyes on me now and raised his arm, preparing to launch a second chunk of gloopy fruit.

'Why aren't they running about?' the child whined. 'I want to see the grotly human doing people-stuff!'

'They're just brainless beastlies, my scrumplet,' its mother replied. 'Revoltus things, if you ask me!'

'Don't even think about it,' I growled, before the goblin kid could throw his next handful of overripe mush. Suddenly, all the fear and panic and sadness at being filched from my own home, the worry that I wouldn't see my **BRILLIANT** family again, and the anger that Grogbah and his stupid cronies had got away with it, exploded inside me. It was like an instant fireball in my belly. I jumped to my feet and roared through the cage bars like I was a bloodthirsty gristle-witch.

'**AAAAAAAAAAGH!**' the pair screamed, scrambling to a safe distance. **'I ATE TWENTY GOBLINS FOR BREAKFAST!'** I howled, clawing the air and snarling with all the fury that was swooshing around in my tummy. **'BUT I COULD STILL MANAGE A FEW MORE!!'**

They didn't stick around for a second longer, let me tell you. Without even glancing back at the cage, the two stumpy tourists tore off through the park, wailing and gnashing as they went.

At any other time it would have been hilarious to see them sprinting away, scattering coupons and attraction tickets, but not just then …

'Well handled, my dear,' Mrs Morkie chuckled.

'Very well handled,' Gully agreed as he sat back up. He searched my face for a smile, only to catch a flash of unhappiness in my eyes again. I couldn't hide it.

'It'll be all right in the end, I promise,' he said. 'We'll be your family now.'

For a second, I thought I was going to burst out

sobbing, but I gritted my toes and clenched my bottom. The last thing I wanted was for one of the goblins outside to see me upset.

'That's right,' Mrs Morkie sighed, scooping me onto her lap and wrapping me in a hairy hug. 'We might be squished like pickled prawks in a jar, but we're pickled prawks together.'

'Exactly!' Gully said, climbing onto Morkie's lap as well and snuggling into her fur next to me. 'You'll get used to zoo life in no time.'

I managed a pathetic smile at Gully and Mrs Morkie, even though I remember secretly thinking there was no way that could **EVER** happen. But the truth is … I suppose it did after a while.

—··◗│◖··— —▶│◀··—

Mushrooms brightened and faded, and days and nights rolled along until I started to lose count of how many had passed by. A week? Two? Maybe three? I had no idea.

In the daytime, when the toadstools all glowed brilliantly, we spent the hours watching the tourists

come and go, clicking their cameras and waving their guidebooks.

Everything ran like clockwork in that horrible place. If Mum was here, she couldn't have organised it better!

On Moondays (that's Monday to you humans) the Grimegorn guards would escort me from my cage to the Predator Parade Theatre, where I'd have to stand while noggin-bonked goblins would take photographs, holler and throw food at me. It was about as glum and dismal a mess as I've ever been in, but I soon learned that if I roared and gave them a bit of a show, I could collect a feast to take back for Viscera, Gully and Mrs Morkie. I'm serious! A few days ago, I caught a whole roasted trog hog, and this morning a particularly spoiled-looking family threw a crustacean-cream cake! Goblins have fancy taste in food!

Then, on Wungleswatch (that's the magical version of Wednesday – don't ask) I would be moved to the big bird-like cage in the centre of the park, so

tourists could get that extra bit closer and have their pictures taken right in front of me.

It was the WORST! I swear! Scaring goblins who were brave enough to walk up to the bars became the only fun thing to do to help while away the hours on those grim days.

And then … in the evenings, after the mushrooms had shrivelled and the customers had gone back to their sewer streets and houses, me, Gully and Mrs Morkie would huddle in the darkness, chatting. I hadn't managed to talk too much about my family yet – it upset me too much – but I don't know what I would have done without my cellmates to cheer me up.

It turned out that Gully was **GREAT** at telling jokes, and Morkie refused to stop trying to tempt Viscera out of her lantern sulking space with stories and promises of cups of imaginary tea.

'Would you like some, deary?' Mrs Morkie would say into the little glowing lamp.

'BOG OFF!' came the angrily squeaked reply, and the candle inside the lantern would be immediately extinguished.

It was always the same, my reader friend. Day after night after day after night. And it looked like it was going to stay that way, until …

THEN THERE WERE FIVE

Mutter … grumble … moan …

I opened one eye and listened for a moment, then wondered if I'd imagined it. I was on Mrs Morkie's knee, snoozing peacefully. Maybe I was still dreaming?

I'd been in Grimegorn for longer than I could keep track of by now. I had taken to counting on the stone walls, scratching notches every day with a little pebble that had been thrown by a goblin tourist, but I still couldn't work it out.

Who could be nattering at this time of night? The tour guides had gone home ages ago, and the night guards only marched about in brutish silence.

Murmur … mumble … groan …

The noise came again, and this time it sounded

much closer. It seemed to be coming from outside the cage.

I sat up groggily and saw that Gully and Mrs Morkie were both quietly dozing. It couldn't be either of them, so I clambered down the side of the cuddlump's hairy leg and crept towards the bars.

I wasn't sure why, but the hairs on the back of my neck started to tingle, and was it me, or did I catch the unmistakeable scent of magical spells on the air? I hadn't smelled that fizzy whiff since the last time I saw Maudlin Maloney. It pricked at my memories of home, waking me fully in an instant. What if … What if my ancient leprechaun friend had finally come to rescue me?

'Hello?' I stammered, peering into the gloom outside. 'Maudlin? Is that you?'

For a second, I could only make out the shape of a nearby bench and the shut-up snack cart that sold toe-cheese popcorn and bunion burgers, but as my troll-eyes adjusted, I spotted a shadowy figure standing in the little stream that flowed near our cage.

Whatever this creature was, its face was hidden deep in the folds of a tattered cloak, but a pair of large orange eyes blinked at me from beneath the hood. They seemed to stare right into my brain, and I caught the smell of sorcery wafting around me again.

I could barely breathe and my skin prickled with goosebumps. There was no way the strange figure could be a goblin – or Maudlin Maloney, for that matter. It was as tall as Dad and incredibly thin.

'Frankie?' a voice whispered behind me. I was so startled my hair nearly stood on end right there and then. I let out an embarrassing yelp as I spun round.

'It's all right! It's just me!' The voice belonged to Gully. He click-clacked a few steps closer, rubbing his eye with the back of his wrist. 'What are you doing?'

'There's someone … something out there, Gully,' I whimpered as a jolt of fear crackled through me. Whatever this creature was, I felt sure it shouldn't be here. 'In the water.'

The faun wrinkled up his forehead in concentration and squinted sleepily out into the darkness.

'Where?'

As if in answer to Gully's question, the creature hopped out of the water and padded over to us, making wet slapping sounds against the pavement with its large frog-like feet that stuck out beneath the cloak.

'Oh!' Gully gasped as he spotted the shadowy figure. I expected him to look as scared and worried as I felt, so I was pretty confused to see a smile spread across his face.

'That's Impya!' he beamed. Then he turned to where Mrs Morkie was snoring and yelled, 'Morkie! Impya's here. Wake up!'

'Blurgh!' Mrs Morkie jolted awake. 'What? Tea, anyone?'

'It's Impya!' Gully cheered again. 'She's here!'

'Ah, lovely,' Mrs Morkie replied, coming to her senses. She shuffled nearer to us on her bottom. 'How nice to have a bit of extra company.'

The thing – Impya – stepped into the candlelight right outside the cell and grunted a greeting.

'I've come to have a nose about,' she said, grabbing the bars with long webbed fingers and sniffing the air. 'The pipes have been echoing with rumours, so I thought I'd come see if all the gossip is true. Has loopy-Latrina really clunked a human?'

'Here I am,' I said to the creature, and she snapped her head towards me.

This close to the cage lanterns, I could make out the lines of Impya's face under the heavy hood. She looked like some kind of froggle with her mottled blotchy skin and those enormous round eyes, but nothing like Mr Croakum back at the hotel. This thing was different to any species of froggle I'd seen before.

'So, this is what all the fuss is about,' she said, inspecting me. 'I never thought I'd see an overling again. It's been over a hundred years. You're so … little.'

Something about this strange animal from the stream filled me with a sense of unease. She stank

of rare hexes and forbidden spells I'd heard Maudlin muttering about.

Clutching a wooden staff covered in hanging bottles and pouches, wearing a cloak dotted with buttons, brooches, trinkets and talismans of all descriptions, she was a magical sight to behold. Mischief oozed from her every pore.

If I've learned anything from spending time with Mankey Old Maloney and all her charms, it probably meant Impya was MEGA tricksy too. Although Mrs Morkie and Gully's excitement at seeing the strange creature made me wonder if she might be as helpful as my leprechaun friend.

'It's squibbly to see you, Impya!' Morkie chuckled.

'Likewise,' the frog-thing answered. Then, to me, 'What are you gawping at, human?'

I hadn't realised I was goggling quite so insanely, and I blinked then looked down at my feet, blushing.

'I'm only twisting your tail,' she rasped. I couldn't tell if it was a cough or a laugh. 'Old Impya is used to it. They all gawk at me, so they do. Pointing and shouting, 'Wretch Wench! Mucus Mother! Slime Wife!" GO BACK TO WHERE YOU CAME FROM! Simpletumps!'

'Oh, my dear!' Mrs Morkie laughed. 'Such names … I don't know where they come up with them. They've all got tiny brains!'

Impya shrugged.

'Nasty small-minded goblins,' Morkie continued. 'Well, don't hang around outside, friend, the guards are on patrol.'

I watched with my heart pounding in my ears as Impya stepped right up to the iron bars and pressed herself against one of the narrow gaps.

'You can't fit through there.' I grimaced. 'It's too small – you'll hurt yourself!'

'Watch this.' Gully beamed, twitching his eyebrows mischievously.

And watch it I did …

There was a slurping squidgy sound and I nearly

cried out with
shock as the bizarre
creature smooshed
herself through the
bars. It was like an
octopus fitting into
the tiny spaces of
a coral reef.

'Ta-dah,' Impya
croaked. In no time
she was next to us
inside the cage,
brushing out the
wrinkles in her cloak
with her speckled
fingers.

'How did you do
that?' I asked,
forgetting my worry
and brimming with excitement
instead. 'That was honkhumptious!'

My thoughts started to race. A magical stranger

appearing out of the night and squishing herself through the bars of our cell was pretty impressive stuff, and … what if Impya was the glimmer of hope I'd been praying for? I've felt guilty about poor Princess Von Tangle ever since we got stuck in Grimegorn, but if this froggle-thing could teach me to squeeze through the cage bars, she might be the key to us getting out of here.

'It's just a talent.' Impya smirked. 'Something I learned. Means I can ramble wherever I like. Stay hidden. Sneak about …'

'You go everywhere, don't you?' Morkie cooed. 'Back and forth and back again.'

'There's nothing I haven't seen on my wandering.' Impya nodded. 'No one can squizzle the Slime Wife in a cage.'

'Well, we're glad you've wandered over to see us again,' said Gully. 'It's been ages.'

'These tired feet have been all over the wuzzled world,' Impya grunted as she sat herself on the stone floor and stretched out her legs. 'I couldn't resist returning to have a look at this young human, though.'

'Have you come across anything interesting lately, dear?' Mrs Morkie asked.

'Armfuls of oddlies. The world is a dark and stupidly place … full of finger-pointers and tongue-clickers …'

'Oh! Tell us **EVERYTHING**!' the cuddlump chuckled, rubbing her hands together. 'It's been yonks and yonkers since we've had news from out there. Any juicy gossipy bits?'

'Hogsplosh to all that!' Impya replied with a crooked smile. 'Nothing but idiumps and prattlers out there! The Slime Wife didn't travel all this way to tell you bedtime stories about snipes in the pipes and gormorous goblins, Morkie! My squeery ears want to hear all about you …' She waved her wooden staff at me and waggled it under my nose. 'You're a long way from home, boy. Something wonksome's happened here …'

'Oh! I'm so glad you said that, Impya!' Mrs Morkie squealed with delight, turning her attention

my way. 'I didn't think it polite to snoop, but I've been itching and scritching to ask about how you ended up here, Frankie ... and the tiny princess.'

'Princess?' snorted Impya.

'She's not too happy,' Mrs Morkie whispered, pointing at the lantern on the wall. 'Stropsy little thing. Piskie royalty. Doesn't come out much.'

'Bah to princesses,' Impya grunted. 'I want to hear your story, overling.'

'Me too!' Gully joined in with a wink. He sat on the floor next to Impya, just far enough away to avoid the pool of green ooze that was spreading out around her like a moat. They didn't call her the Slime Wife for nothing.

'That's settled, then. Now start from the beginning,' Impya croaked. 'And don't leave **ANYTHING** out!'

STORIES IN THE DARK

After what must have been weeks of living crumped up and miserable in Grimegorn, I realised I still hadn't told my new friends why me and Viscera were there in the first place. I had attempted it a few times when we'd been joking and telling tales late at night, but it made me feel too sad and teary to talk about, so I just gave up.

I knew my cellmates' stories almost by heart. Gully had been grabbed while he was taking a nap from his faun clan's Great Grecian Hinkapoot Hunt, and Mrs Morkie had regaled us loads of times with stories of the night she had wandered into Gradibash when she was on a sightseeing holiday in the Underneath. Stupid Queen Latrina had mistaken the kindly cuddlump for a razor-toothed pudgenut and thrown her into the zoo nearly seventy years ago!

At first, the idea of retelling everything that had happened to me over the past **CRAZY** summer made me feel all wimbly and I wasn't even sure I could get the words out. I'd done my best to try and not think about my beautiful-bonkers family and the hotel too much lately. It always left me down-in-the-dumples whenever I did.

'Ummm,' I mumbled with a trembling voice. 'I … Well …'

'Yes?' Morkie said with a grin. 'That's a good start. What else?'

'You see … I … There was … ummm … I don't …' It was no use. I could already feel my eyes filling with tears. If I spoke one more word, I knew I'd be blubbing like a blurtle in seconds.

'What is it, Frankie?' Gully asked. 'Are you all right?'

'Get on with it!' Impya grunted. 'I travelled for moons and noons to see you.'

This was it. I could feel a great big sob heaving

its way into my chest. I was going to burst out crying and embarrass myself in three ... two ...

'BANISTER BOY!'

I looked up, surprised to see that Viscera Von Tangle had wriggled her way out of the lantern on the wall and was perched on the edge of an uneven brick. It had been days since she'd shown her face and my heart jumped into my throat at the sight of the piskie princess giving me a nod and a little smile.

'Oh, how jibbly!' Morkie sighed when she saw Viscera. 'The little'un's come to have a listen too. There she is, Impya. Look!'

'Greetings, Piskie Princess,' Impya said.

'Not interested!' Viscera replied, refusing to acknowledge anyone but me.

'Oh, come and join us, Victor … Visscee … Vitsy …' Mrs Morkie continued, but the princess wasn't listening. Instead, the pouting piskie glared at me then pointed to something near Mrs Morkie's enormous furry bottom.

'What?' I asked as Viscera continued to jab her finger towards it.

'Use your eyes, quarterling!' she snapped.

I looked closer at where Morkie was sitting and spotted the corner of something purple sticking out from beneath her.

'What is it, dear?' the cuddlump asked, shifting about. 'Have I squashed something?'

'It's … It's …' I squinted my eyes and tried to figure out what I was looking at. 'It's my jacket!'

After all this time, I'd completely forgotten about my bell-hop uniform. I'd folded it up as a pillow on my first night in the cage and hadn't seen it since.

'Oh, good gracicles!' Mrs Morkie chuckled. 'I do apologise, Frankie. I must have shuffled my bottlies on top of it by mistake.'

'It's all right,' I said, as Morkie heaved herself up for a moment.

Yanking the jacket out from beneath the cuddlump, I lifted it and turned back to Viscera. 'Is this what you meant, Princess?'

'Your top pocket!' the piskie squeaked at me, and my jaw nearly fell off and clattered across the floor.

In a fraction of a second, I realised what Viscera was talking about.

My fingers wriggled into the folds of the purple uniform pocket and grazed the hard corner of a creased photograph. I plucked it out and unfolded it with a rush of happiness. In all the craziness, I'd completely forgotten that it was even there. **'MY FAMILY!'** I blurted, grinning through my tears.

I don't know how to describe the feeling, my reader friend. Seeing Mum, Dad, Nancy and Maudlin smiling back at me almost made it feel as if they were here with me in the cage. Suddenly my need to sob was replaced with the urge to jabber on about these **BRILLIANT** people and our hotel home for hours. I could have talked all night. Just saying their names gave me a warm and fuzzy feeling in my belly, and it was **HUMDEFFEROUS**!

'I'm ready to tell my story.' I beamed to my captive audience.

'Oh, wait one minkly-moment!' Impya interrupted. She fumbled with a tiny glass vial that hung from the end of her staff, cracked it in her palm and we all watched as a purple cloud of shimmering mist rose into the air between us.

'What's that?' I asked as the old familiar smell of magic filled my nostrils.

'A chronicloud,' Impya answered. 'Used by magical minstrels from here to the earthly ends. Make sure you speak directly into it …'

'Go on, Frankie,' said Gully with a grin. 'I've seen one of these before. It's fun!'

Taking another look at my family's photograph in my hand, I stepped closer to the purple smoke and …

'Well, I should begin with **The Nothing To See Here Hotel**,' I said, then gasped in amazement as a sparkling vision of my fabulous home appeared inside the chronicloud.

'Isn't it grumptious!' Morkie cooed.

'It's beamly,' I laughed. 'I live there with …'

In no time wispy images of Mum and Dad and everyone I could think of to describe were dancing through the air before us.

I explained to Morkie, Gully and Impya how it had all started way back on the night of the storm, telling them about Muggerty Manglejaw, and Grogbah's dramatic entrance through the grumbling lawn. I detailed how the goblins had taken over the hotel, and the surprise arrival of Captain Calamitus Plank and his daughter, Tempestra, on board their ship, the *Blistered Barnacle*.

'Well, I never!' Morkie hooted as the glowing mirage of Captain Plank's galleon glided across our cage on a magical wave.

When I got to the part about Maudlin Maloney crashing through the sky-door in her chicken-powered lepre-caravan, and the ferocious blizzard that engulfed the hotel, and our yeti friends' arrival,

everyone was laughing and cheering with wonder.

'All that happened this summer!?' asked Gully, scratching his head. 'Incrudible!'

'That's not all!' I went on. 'At the same time as the yetis, a gnomad arrived with a talking magpie called Jindabim.'

It was at that moment that Impya jerked and sat up straighter, leaning in like she didn't want to miss a single word of my story. Well, who could blame her? It is a whoppsy good one, after all. Especially with the use of her handy chronicloud.

'Go on, boy,' she rasped. 'What happened next?'

'Dark and weirdly things started happening around the hotel,' I said. 'Thorn tendrils grew all over reception from a dead plant, and Maudlin's collection of shrunken heads came to life, ruining our Trogmanay feast!'

'What else?'

'At first, we all thought Maloney had done it to punish us for all the snow, but it turned out to be the gnomad and his flea-bitten bird. It was really my great-great-uncle in disguise!'

'This is better than any of the Greek myths my clan used to tell,' Gully laughed.

'Why was your great-great-uncle in disguise?' asked Morkie. 'Don't stop now, dear! It's exciterous!'

'It's mega long and confusing,' I said. 'But it turns out my great-great-uncle was cursed by a **DISGUSTING** graveghast when he was a kid and he's loop-de-loop crazy with anger about it. He wanted to have revenge on my family by breaking the invisibility spells and exposing the hotel to the human world.'

'The little rottler!' Morkie scoffed. 'You could have ended up in a zoo! Oh … umm … well, another zoo!'

'And what was his name?' Impya asked. She was barely blinking.

I reached back inside my jacket pocket and plucked out a second photograph. It was the portrait of my great-great-uncle and his mother, Olympia Nocturne, from Grandad Abe's office in the Briny Ballroom.

'His name was Oculus,' I said, and felt my spine

tingle as his ghostly apparition appeared in the magical cloud.

'Here – this is him, and his mum. She was cursed by the graveghast too, but was never seen again. No one knows what happened to her. I've kept their photo ever since I found it. Sort of felt sorry for them, I suppose. Imagine stumbling across a gut-grunching death fairy!'

'Show me the real photograph!' Impya ordered.

I handed it to her and she snatched it, staring at it thoughtfully.

'This is a horrible story,' she mumbled, her wide eyes darting over the grim faces.

'Oh, I'm sorry,' I said, suddenly worrying that I might have insulted Impya. Who knows? With the scent of magic so strong around her, maybe she was part-graveghast, just like I'm part-troll.

'Horrible and sad,' Impya hissed.

'You'll NEVER guess what happened next!' I whooped, waving my arms for dramatic effect. I decided it was probably a good idea to hurry on with the story before the frog-lady cursed me too.

'My family defeated Oculus good and proper, and now his body is frozen in a block of ice in the Himalayas and his spectril is safely hidden away on the highest shelf of the hotel's library in a jar!'

'**AMAZING!**' Gully cried, clapping his hands.

'We'd never have survived without the help of my great-great-great-grandad, Abraham Banister!'

Impya suddenly grunted and the photograph in her slimy fingers exploded in a tiny burst of flames.

'My photo!' I yelped as it crumbled into an instant snowfall of ash.

'Oops!' Impya replied with a muddled expression on her face. It was somewhere between scared and completely shocked. 'My mistake.'

'Why did you do that?' I snapped. 'It's the only picture I have of Oculus!'

'Magical hiccup,' Impya answered quickly. She was leaning so far forwards, I thought she might topple onto the floor. 'Don't stop now, boy. You were talking about Abraham Banister!'

'Have you heard of him?' I asked. Something about the way Impya was staring at me told me not to grumble too much about the destroyed picture. She was tricksy for certain. 'Grandad Abe is pretty famous. He was an explorer back in his day.'

Impya didn't say anything.

'Mrs Morkie has heard of him, haven't you?'

'Oh, yes! He was a marvellous chap, your great-great-great-grandad,' Morkie replied. 'Lovely!'

We all looked at Impya and waited for her answer. She ignored us and glared at Abe's face in the chronicloud for what felt like far too long.

'Bah!' she finally snorted with a shrug, before wafting her hand and making the purple smoke disappear. 'Human names all sound the same to me. My mucus-memories aren't what they used to be.'

With that, Impya picked up her wooden stick and clambered to her feet.

'I'm leaving now,' she said. 'I came here for exciting stories from the human world, and instead I get this sad tearmongering.'

'But you didn't get to the part with me!' Viscera Von Tangle squeaked from her perch on the wall. 'That's the best bit!'

'I don't have time,' Impya replied flatly.

'How dare you, you sluggerous skrunt?' Viscera balked. 'I'm royalty, I'll have you know! You should make time!'

'The Slime Wife has listened to enough for one night,' Impya shot back, shaking her head. 'These old ears wanted to hear about the boy – not useless piskies and cursed families.'

'**USELESS? HOW RUDE!**' Princess Von Tangle looked like someone had smacked her round her tiny face.

'Off so soon?' Morkie asked sadly. 'You've only just got here.'

'The Slime Wife never stays in one place too long,' Impya croaked. 'It's time to be off.'

'Are you going home?' I asked, still concerned about why she hadn't liked my story. I'd hoped she would stick around for longer. That way I could try and steer the conversation towards plans for escaping.

'I don't have a home,' Impya scoffed. 'I'm going back to my wandering. There's no home for a

creature like me. I'm one of the broken things of the world. Thrown away and forgotten, I just keep going ...'

I watched as Impya hobbled over to the cage bars on her long froggy-feet and I could feel panic spreading through my veins. If she left, I'd probably never have the opportunity to ask her again. That was the moment, right then, before the thought had even turned into a proper idea in my head, I opened my mouth and I shouted ...

· 27 ·

VERY DEEP POCKETS

'WAIT!' I yelled.

Impya stopped in her tracks, then turned and studied me with her large orange eyes.

'Are you all right, Frankie?' Mrs Morkie asked. 'I'm not sure shouting is very sensible, dear. You'll alert the goblin guards.'

'Impya!' I walked right up to the frog-thing and didn't even care when I felt my shoes slip in the slime that was pooling around her feet.

'What?' she asked suspiciously, looking at me in a way that told me she already knew what I was going to say.

'Take us with you!'

There was a second of silence as the Slime Wife mulled over my request, then she laughed in my face.

'You've gone stuperish!'

'I mean it!' I snapped. 'Help us to get out of here. Let us come with you.'

'I can't!' Impya replied.

'But you can squeeze through the bars! We all saw you do it. Show us the spell and we'll be able to leave this place with you,' I begged. 'Please!'

'Don't be so brain-bungled,' Impya said. 'It isn't a spell. It's just something I can do.'

'I don't believe you!' My heart pounded in my chest. If there was a moment to escape Grimegorn, this was it. It wasn't every day a magical creature who could slip through the bars showed up in your prison cell. This was our chance, I just knew it. 'I smelled magic on you as soon as you were near. You can help us, I know you can.'

'I'm not that kind of magical,' Impya grunted. 'I'm enchanted, not an enchanter. I can't just put a spell on you to squish your way out of here.'

'Please, Impya!' I pleaded as a horrible sinking feeling crept over me. 'You've got to help us. Please ... **PLEASE!!!**'

'Frankie.' Gully placed a hand on my shoulder and looked at me with sad eyes. 'It's no use. Impya can't do it.'

I stared at the frog-woman and knew from the unexpected sorrowful expression on her face that she was telling the truth.

'I'm sorry, boy,' she muttered. 'The only way of getting out of this cage is with the keys, and they'll be jangling about on Captain Grumpwhistle's belt as we speak. There's nothing I can do.'

Impya turned to leave again and I racked my brain, trying to think of something to say that might change her mind. I opened my mouth to call after her, but it was Viscera Von Tangle who broke the silence before I could utter a word.

'Is that all you need?' she peeped. 'Just a stupidous key? Why didn't you say so?'

We all turned to look at the princess as she dug one of her matchstick-sized arms into the folds of her frilly caterpillar-silk dress and started rummaging in a pocket.

'**GOT IT!**' Viscera cheered, as she pulled out a large brass key. It was twice as long as she was tall. 'I'm not so useless now, am I, Slime Wife? Haha!'

I walked over to where the piskie was standing on the uneven brickwork and took the key from her. It was … it was … I recognised it immediately.

'This is the key to Ooof's cellar,' I said, turning it over in my hand. 'It went missing just after we got back from the bottom of the sea.'

'Indeed!' Viscera laughed. 'And now we will use it to escape. Princess Von Tangle has saved everything.'

'Oh, Princess,' I said. I couldn't help but feel sorry for her. 'You don't understand. This isn't the right one.'

'Not right?' she barked, then shoved her hand back into the frilly petticoats of her ballgown. 'How about this?'

Viscera brandished the ink pen that Mum used to sign guests into the hotel at the reception desk. She was furious when it went missing and had blamed the home-sweet-home hobs for over-tidying.

'This is the answer to all our problems!'

'No ...' I felt mean, letting the princess down again. 'That won't work either.'

'Peskie piskies and their bottomless pockets,' Impya grumbled. 'Always stealing things that don't belong to them.'

'This? Or this?' Viscera went on. 'How about this?' In only a few seconds the princess had yanked a bent teaspoon, half a pencil, the little whisk that Nancy used to froth the mugs of hot chunklet, a rusty nail, a blue toothbrush that Dentina Molar had reported missing, and one of Hoggit's dragon chew-sticks from the folds of her sparkly dress.

'Goodness,' Mrs Morkie chuckled. 'You've quite

the collection there, dear. We've got a thumb-sized thief on our hands.'

'I know!' Viscera cooed. She reached into her pocket again and pulled out a twisted piece of metal with a small skull-shaped bead at one end. 'This is the one!'

'That's ...' I took the strange object from her and examined it. 'That's the skell-a-phone key!!'

Viscera stared at me blankly.

'We never found it again after Grandad Abe's ghost arrived in the kitchen! Maudlin was SO cross!'

The piskie princess shrugged.

'Well, now we can use it to get out of here!' she said. **'LET'S GO, BANISTER BOY!'**

'The poor little thing,' Mrs Morkie sighed. 'When you're that small, I don't suppose you ever really need to grasp the way locks and keys work.'

'No good?' Viscera asked. 'I have more!'

Next the tiny princess pulled out a stripy drinking straw, an old twig and a chopstick.

'Yes?' she asked optimistically.

'I'm afraid not,' I answered.

'I've had enough of this nonsense,' Impya croaked. 'Goodbye to you all. May you fare well in this muck-dump.'

It felt like our last shred of a chance was leaving with the Slime Wife and I barely noticed when Viscera yanked out one last object from her pocket.

'This is the one!'

If what the princess was clutching hadn't glinted brilliant green in the candlelight and caught our attention, I think I would have ignored her and curled up for a cry on the cage floor.

'What was that?' Gully gasped.

We all turned back to face Viscera. I looked at what the little figure was holding and my neck prickled with goosebumps.

'What *was* that?' Impya echoed. Even she seemed intrigued by the thin sliver of jade in the piskie's hands.

'Don't know,' Viscera replied. 'Found it in a pile of dirt sweepings outside the hotel dining room. I like shiny things. Saved it before those yucksome dust pooks ate it.'

The green object glinted again and I thought I might burst into happy tears for a change.

There, clutched in her tiny arms, was one of the jade handles from the magical knife and fork set we used on special occasions. They were bewitched with the power to shrink any guest down to the size of a minklemeat nugget. We thought they'd been lost after Nancy snapped them to save us all from the marauding shrunken heads at our disastrous Trogmanay feast!

'Princess, you've saved us …' I wheezed.

'Oh, good!' Viscera replied, wedging her hands on her hips. 'Shall we go, then?'

'HONKSWALLOP!'

'I'm not sure about this,' Mrs Morkie stammered. 'I've been in the clunk for seventy years at least. What if it's all different out there in the great wudgie world?'

'You can do it, Morkie!' Gully squeaked. He had already shrunk down to the size of Viscera Von Tangle and was standing next to her on the wonky brick in the middle of the wall. 'It's actually quite fun!'

'He's right,' I reassured the giant cuddlump with a huge grin. I was practically buzzing with excitement. 'Just think, you'll be able to stand up. You'll be free to stretch your legs!'

'Good gracicles,' Mrs Morkie chuckled. 'I hadn't thought of that.'

'Mum and Dad will find you a warm place at the hotel, I know they will.'

'Me!? Staying in a wiffly place like **The Nothing To See Here Hotel?**' Morkie fanned her face with her enormous fuzzy hand. 'I can't believe it. Will there be tea?'

'More tea than you could ever drink!' I smiled. 'And squillions of different kinds!'

'Oh, I'm as giddy as a gunkle!'

'Then get on with it!' Viscera moaned.

'Oh, yes,' Morkie said, trying to calm herself down. She looked at me with an expression as if to say, *Show me what to do* ...

'Here.' I handed Mrs Morkie the jade cutlery handle and she took it carefully between two of her stumpy claws. 'Now all you have to do is bang it on the ground and shout, *HONKSWALLOP!*'

'Righty-ho,' Morkie muttered. She scooted along on her bottom to where the stone floor was a little more even and raised her hand. 'Wish me luck.'

With that, the gargantuan creature brought her hairy hand down with a thump and shouted the special word. There was a fizzing noise and the air seemed to pop and sizzle as Morkie vanished down to the size of … of … well, she wasn't exactly as small as Viscera and Gully, but she was small enough.

'Oh, bust my boogles!' she cried. The giant cuddlump was now about the size of a moss gremlin and she started spinning around the cage, hopping and twirling. 'I can stand! I can straighten my limbies without hitting the walls. I'm as free as a frumplet!'

Now it was my turn.

I quickly put on my purple jacket, kneeled on the cold stone and picked up the slither of jade that Morkie had dropped when she started prancing about.

'HONKSWALLOP!' I shouted as I banged the green object down, instantly feeling magic zig-zagging around my fingers. In an instant, the ground rushed up to meet me, and there I was – the size of a thumb for the first time since Trogmanay.

RUN FOR IT!

'Bleurgh!' Viscera Von Tangle walked across the floor stones towards me and grimaced. 'You're a lot uglier up close.'

I slightly wished I could say the same about her, but it was **AMAZING** seeing the piskie princess in so much detail. Her hair looked like it was laced with silver threads and the puffy caterpillar-silk ballgown glistened with pinks and greens like the shell of a beetle as she swished.

'Frankie!' Gully yipped, as he flung his arms round my neck and smiled so widely I thought his face might crack. 'This is TERRIFIC!'

'It takes a bit of getting used to,' I said to my faun friend. 'But we don't have much time. With only one jade handle, and a broken one at that, I don't know how long this spell will last.'

'What do we do now, my lumplet?' Mrs Morkie thudded over. It was funny that we'd all shrunk but she was still so much bigger than us.

I turned and looked up at where Impya was standing near the bars of the cage, a look of total confusion on her face.

'Okay, Impya,' I said. 'Let's go …'

The Slime Wife stared down at us, blinked a few times, then opened her mouth and …

'I DIDN'T AGREE TO THIS!!'

'Aaaagh!' Morkie and Gully cowered, smacking their hands over their ears.

'Oh, darling,' Morkie wailed. 'Quieter! Much, much quieter.'

Impya rolled her eyes, then got down on her knees and whispered.

'I didn't agree to any of this,' she hissed. 'You didn't ask me before you tinkered yourselves all tiny. Impya wanders alone!'

'Impya, this is our only chance. Please help us,' I said in my most serious voice. 'You can't leave us here for ever.'

The Slime Wife thought for a moment, eyeing us the way someone eyes the pieces of a game of chess, planning their next move.

'Too dangerous,' she finally said. 'You'll be grunched, or squelched, or scrumbled.'

She shifted as though she was about to stand up,

when Viscera Von Tangle rushed in front of me.

'Now, you listen to me, you frogspawny old **FRUMPLE!**' the princess hollered. 'Everyone is small enough to fit through the bars of this stinksome cell now, and you know the way out of Gradibash, don't you?'

'Like the back of my hackled hands,' Impya muttered.

'Then you're going to help us get out of this rottly zoo and away from here, or I'll send out an order for hordes of piskies to yank on your yungles and prickle you with pins for the rest of your life!'

Impya gawped at the tiny barking princess.

'**DO YOU UNDERSTAND???**' Viscera shrieked.

There was a long pause, until …

'Fine,' Impya said. 'But don't blame me if you get caught and cut up into snacks for that crunkodile down at the palace …'

In no time, the Slime Wife had placed me and

Gully in one of the pouches that hung from her wooden staff. Viscera was standing in a little glass bottle that dangled next to us, and Mrs Morkie was trotting along close behind Impya's heels.

'Stay very quiet,' Impya whispered as she squeezed out through the cage and into the night. 'The guards around here are bored and dangerous. They'll grind us into grunion gravy if they catch us.'

I watched with my heart pounding in my chest as the Slime Wife stole silently into the darkness, crossed the little stream, and began to make her way around the open garden at the centre of Grimegorn.

Whenever I had been marched off to the Predator Parade Theatre, I was always surrounded by armed goblins and chattering tourists, so I'd never had the chance to properly look into the other exhibits before. I couldn't believe the size of Queen Latrina's magical menagerie. There were **HUNDREDS** of creatures in this place.

We passed a fenced pen filled with stomping dungles, a cage with a sleeping nifflehog inside, and even three massive water jars containing a mergully, an anemononk and a family of kulpies.

There were petting areas with grumplings and garvils, cages of puddle nymphs and hobyahs, and a vast pool filled with a slowly pulsating hungletub.

'All these unfortunate magicals,' Gully said as he peered into the shadows. 'What do we do about them? Can they be rescued?'

'We can't do anything like that until we've escaped ourselves,' I said. 'Mum and Dad will know what to do once we're back at the hotel.'

Gully nodded but didn't reply.

'That's enough jabbering, you two,' Impya whispered as we passed a boggart-meat burger stall. 'Even tiny voices can get us caught in all this silence.'

The Slime Wife grabbed Mrs Morkie by the hand and pressed herself into the narrow shadow behind a 'GIFTSHOP THIS WAY' signpost as a battalion of goblin guards suddenly marched across our path. We all held our breaths as the squat things clomped off in the direction of the polar pludges, and Impya didn't dare to make a single movement until they were long out of sight.

'See what I mean?' she hissed.

Once the way was clear, we headed past the grizzigulp enclosure, round the pook pens and finally stopped at a large metal grate where the stream trickled its way out through the wall.

'Nearly there,' Impya whispered, squishing her way inside. 'Hold on to your haunches.'

We passed along a stinky drainage tunnel and through a second grate on the other side, and then …

FREEDOM!

We were outside the high windowless walls of Grimegorn with the wonderful sight of Gradibash spreading out below us, shimmering and sparkling as it slept.

'We did it!' I cheered. For the first time in weeks, **The Nothing To See Here Hotel** felt within reach. 'I knew we'd get out of here.'

'Honkhumptious!' Morkie gasped as she looked down at the great city. 'It's been so long!'

'We're not safe yet,' Gully said. 'We've got to get down to the docks without being spotted.'

'It's all downhill from here,' I replied. 'Everyone's snoring in their beds. If we keep quiet and stick to the shadows, we can make it there in no time.'

'Exactly,' Viscera joined in. 'Banister boy is right. Slime Wife, ONWARDS!'

We glanced up to Impya, towering above us.

It was clear from the look on her giant face that she had no intention of going into the city.

'Please, Impya!' I pleaded before she'd even opened her mouth. 'Just down to the water's edge.'

'I got you out of the clunk,' she croaked. 'Impya stops here.'

'Oh, come now, dear,' said Mrs Morkie, trying to hide the look of worry on her face. 'It's not far, and you know the way better than any of us. Please …'

'I can't be seen in the city. They threw rocks last time! It's back to wandering the warrens and plodding the pipes for me.' Impya shook her head, then lowered the end of her staff to the road so that me, Gully and Viscera could climb out of the pouch and bottle. 'Go quick and go quiet.'

I stumbled onto the giant cobbles and helped Gully climb down after me. Being the size of a piskie made even the tiniest of drops seem daunting.

'Is everyone in one piece?' I asked, checking that Viscera and Morkie were all right.

'I've never felt more alive,' Viscera chuckled.

'Can you at least point us in the right—' I turned to where Impya had been standing only seconds before. She was gone.

'That's that, then,' Gully stammered nervously.

'Does anyone have a map?' Morkie whimpered.

TROLLEY DASH

Being only as tall as a human thumb, and without Impya to help us get through the city, left an empty and nervous feeling in the pit of my belly.

'We just have to head downhill, I think,' I said to Mrs Morkie. 'We'll reach the Great Cistern Lake eventually. I'm sure of it.'

'Which way do you think we should go?' Gully asked.

I took a moment and looked at our options. To our right, Ramscottle Street led towards the palace of Queen Latrina. That was the route Grumpwhistle and his grizzly guards had taken when I was first brought to Grimegorn.

'This way leads straight to Latrina,' I thought out loud. 'I don't fancy getting any closer to that horrible glob-gob than we have to.'

'What about this?' Gully said, pointing to the left, at the only other route we could take. It was a steep and narrow lane that snaked off through a ramshackle part of town.

Mrs Morkie wandered closer to the mouth of the lane and inspected the signpost that pointed along it.

'Gutterplug Alley,' she read. 'What do you think, Frankie?'

'Let's go,' I replied. 'Anything is better than heading towards Queen Latrina.'

'I CAN'T WALK ALL THAT WAY!' Viscera Von Tangle huffed as we were about to set off. 'I'm royalty! A princess doesn't go rambling down alleyways to skuzzly old docks, I'll have you know.'

'Oh,' Mrs Morkie said, confused. 'How do they get about, then?'

'A princess is carried!'

'Ah, righty.' Morkie rolled her eyes. 'We're all teensy-squeensy, but I'm bigger than you three titchies. Why don't you climb on my back and I'll carry you all? We'll get to that dock in a jif—'

'I'VE GOT IT!' I suddenly blurted, making the miniature-sized cuddlump jump. 'Sorry, Morkie, I didn't mean to scare you.'

'That's all right, dear,' she smiled. 'But … erm … what have you got?'

I'd only put my bell-hop jacket back on right before shrinking, and I'd not been concentrating enough to think about all the other trinkets and tats I had stuffed in my pockets. Reaching inside, I shifted my fingers past the folded photographs and …

'Here!' I grinned, pulling out a little disk of coiled metal. 'I forgot this was even in here.'

'What is it?' asked Gully.

'Is it a penny?' Morkie joined in.

'It's the room-service trolley!' I said. 'It'll get us down to the docks in a tinkle of the time.'

Mrs Morkie frowned at me and felt my forehead.

'I think you might be a little exhausted, my lumplet.'

'No, no, you don't understand,' I said, handing the

cuddlump the silvery disk. 'I'm not bonkers! It's enchanted to swizzle up small when it's not being used. You just have to click the centre to uncurl it.'

'How marvellous!' Morkie giggled. 'Go on, then.' She went to pass the trolley-disk back to me, but I stopped her.

'I mustn't,' I said. 'The trolley unravels to exactly the right size for the person who's using it. If I press the button, it'll turn into a tiny thing and we won't all fit on. You're much bigger than us, Morkie. You do it.'

'Hmmmm,' the cuddlump mumbled. 'Let's have a look, then ...'

There was a small *CHINK* as her hairy thumb clicked the centre of the silver disk and it immediately uncurled into a cart that was about half the size of what it would be back at the hotel.

'That's splendifferous!' Mrs Morkie gasped. 'Your coach awaits you, Princess!'

'About blunking time!' Viscera snipped back.

With that, Morkie lifted us all onto the top of the trolley, stepped up onto the back of it and pushed us off with one foot.

'What if we crash?' Gully asked as we neared the top of the steep alleyway. He grabbed the lip of the tray nervously.

'Don't panic,' I smiled, hurrying over, and clutched the little rail too. 'Part of the spell is that it can't topple over. All we have to do hold on tight and …'

'WEEEEEEEEEEEEEEEEEEEEEEEEEE!'

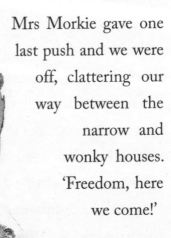

Mrs Morkie gave one last push and we were off, clattering our way between the narrow and wonky houses. 'Freedom, here we come!'

ESCAPE!

'Faster, Furball!' Viscera Von Tangle cooed as we whizzed round another bend in the alleyway. **'GET A MOVE ON!'**

'All right! All right!' Mrs Morkie huffed and puffed behind us. She gave another push with one foot, like someone on a human skateboard, and before long the trolley was hurtling along at a brain-boggling speed.

On either side of us, the dark and sleeping goblin dwellings were practically a blur. Houses and little boutiques, public baths and food shops all raced past as we reached the bottom of the winding lane with an enormous jolt.

Suddenly we were on a wide deserted boulevard of fancy-looking goblin fashion houses and museums.

'I know this place!' I whooped. We had emerged onto Hungdunkem Avenue. 'We're going in the right direction! Head for **THAT**, Morkie!' I pointed to the towering Gradibashi Opera House in the distance, remembering that it stood right next to the docks.

'We're going to make it,' Gully beamed at me. 'We're actually going to escape this dreadful city.'

I smiled back at my faun friend and felt a tingle of hope creep up my spine. Just the thought of seeing Mum and Dad again made me giddy with excitement. I'd already decided that the very first thing I was going to do once we arrived at **The Nothing To See Here Hotel** was to go straight to my room and hug Hoggit, my pet pygmy soot-dragon. Gully would just love him, I knew it …

'Ummmm.'

Viscera caught my attention and I turned to see what her worried whine was all about.

'Am I losing my plonkers or did the buildings just change colour, Banister boy?'

I glanced around the city and … Viscera was

right. What had been shadowy, sleepy streets had started to glow in an eerie blue light.

'**OH, NO!**' Morkie yelped behind us. '**THE TOADSTOOLS! THEY'RE WAKING UP — IT MUST BE MORNING!**'

My excitement and hope turned to a feeling of dread as the whole of Gradibash emerged into view. All around us the giant mushrooms that grew on every street corner got brighter and brighter.

'Don't stop!' I yelled to Mrs Morkie as we careered round the bend onto Prawk Prong Street, then zipped across onto Snootle Boulevard. Suddenly there were goblins emerging on the pavements as they opened the fronts of their shops and restaurants.

'Aaaaagh!' a flamboyantly-styled goblinette screeched as we zoomed past her. She was putting a sign out on the pavement advertising her relaxation mud spa, and our trolley bounced straight over it, making her **topple backwards onto her doorstep.** 'RUMPSCALLIONS! ROTTLERS!'

By the time we passed the opera house, the toadstools were fully lit and we were in plain view to the waking public.

More and more goblins were walking out onto the streets and, as if from nowhere, there were carts and omnibuses trundling into our path.

'Look! Escapees!'

'GET OUT OF THE WAY!'

'CALL THE GOBLIN GUARD!'

I winced as we tore straight underneath a double-decker omnibus being pulled by a harnessed foozle. The room-service trolley narrowly missed its huge wheels as it zipped out the other side and continued to speed downhill towards the docks.

'We can still make it!' Gully cried as Morkie swerved the trolley just in time to miss a little line of terrified goblin children heading to school in their matching uniforms. 'There's still … oh no! Oh no! **OH NO!**'

I looked at Gully and saw that he was suddenly twice as tall as I was.

'The shrinking spell!' I yelled. **'It's wearing off!'** A second later, I could feel my arms and legs stretching and warping.

'OH, BLUNKERS!' Morkie howled as she suddenly grew so tall, she couldn't keep hold of the trolley. I turned just in time to see her trip and fall onto her front in the middle of the road. There was a loud **POP** and she exploded into her full size, putting both her massive feet through the front of an art gallery wall.

The room-service trolley may have been enchanted not to topple over or crash, but it wasn't protected from buckling under the weight of a quarterling and a faun child as they scrabbled to stay on top of it.

When Morkie had uncurled the squeaky thing to the correct size, she hadn't been much bigger than Hoggit, and I felt a shudder as the little wheels bent and broke beneath us.

Before I could shout, 'HOLD ON!' there was a squeal and I rolled across the cobblestones with a painful *HUMPH!*

'Gully,' I murmured, my face squidged against the ground. 'Are you all right?'

'I think so …' he groaned from a little way off.

'Viscera?' I wheezed. 'Are you …?'

'**NO, I AM NOT!**' her piddly voice barked right next to my ear. 'Get up and look, Banister boy!'

I slowly raised my head and focused on the pointy tip of a spear that was hovering just above my head.

I followed it upwards until I saw a stumpy green hand, then a suit of blood-red goblin armour, then the sneering face of Captain Pugnacious Grumpwhistle.

'**Well**,' he said, raising one bristly eyebrow. 'What have we got here?'

SO, THIS IS THE END?

In seconds, there were goblin guards all around us.

'Thought you'd just wander out of here, did you?' Captain Grumpwhistle laughed cruelly as he snatched up Viscera Von Tangle and stuffed her into a pouch on his belt. Then he seized the back of my collar and hoisted me to my feet. **'No one escapes Grimegorn on my watch!'**

I wriggled in the hulking goblin's grasp and turned just enough to see Gully struggling with Flott and Lickspittle. They'd snared him with trap-lace and I could see my faun friend was quickly learning that the more you struggle, the tighter it gets.

'Let us go!' Gully yelled, but his captors only snickered and jeered at him. 'Let us GO!'

'Not on your nelly, you snizzly spit-stain!' Flott guffawed.

A little further up the street, I could see Mrs Morkie contending with her own gaggle of guards. There must have been twenty of the blighters and they were each clutching their own lengths of horrible gold rope that coiled round the poor cuddlump's legs, arms and middle.

'**Frankie!**' she cried, catching my eye.

It was dreadful to watch Mrs Morkie being tied up by those gruzzly little grimlies. She was too kind and cuddly to fight. If the huge creature had been born for anything but snuggling, she could have defeated every goblin guard in Gradibash with a few swats and stomps of her enormous hands and feet. She could squish the entire city in a matter of minutes!

'**Clonk 'em, Morkie!**' I shouted, but it was no use. I could already hear her offering to make the bullyish brutes some tea.

Just like our days back in Grimegorn, we were paraded through the streets while nosy goblins gawked and hollered, throwing food and calling us names. All the commotion had drawn a gigantic crowd, and the stumpy citizens of the great sewer-city lined the pavements, trying to get a good view of us.

'Look this way!'

'And this way! OVER HERE!'

Reporters from the local goblin newspapers, the *Sunday Grimes* and the *Observerator*, took our photographs as we were dragged back towards the top of Hungdunkem Avenue and left on to The Yelps.

I didn't even have to wonder where Captain Grumpwhistle and his flunkies were taking us. I knew already. In no time we were crossing the Just-About-In-The-Middle Bridge and Queen Latrina's palace was looming ahead of us.

This was it. All my hopes of seeing **The Nothing To See Here Hotel** again were over. The BONKERS ruler of Gradibash may have thrown me into a zoo for a first offence, but there was NO WAY I'd be so lucky this time.

I flinched as the thought of being grunched by

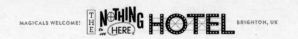
Doris the colossal crocodile slobbered its way across my mind.

There was no doubt about it.

We were absolutely done for.

THE POODLY PLAZA

By the time we'd reached the far side of the Just-About-In-The-Middle-Bridge, the clamour and noise of the crowds was echoing off the great cistern walls and the entire city was vibrating.

Big boomy trumpets were being blown from the watchtowers that surrounded the lake's edge, waking everyone, and a regimental band had collected to bang drums and honk on horns.

'LOOK! COME SEE!' Captain Grumpwhistle hollered over the gathering throng of nosy goblins as we were carried past the front of the palace. 'IT'S THE PERFECT MORNING FOR A FLUSHING!!'

A flushing? I'd forgotten about that particular punishment!

Ahead of us, I could see an open town square with a raised wooden platform at the far end. Beyond it was the gaping mouth of an enormous rusted sewer-pipe that gurgled and spluttered like a hungry monster.

'**FRANKIE!**' I heard Mrs Morkie yell as we were dragged towards the horrible thing. 'I'm not quite sure this is what you had planned! I think it's gone wrong!'

'You're right about one thing!' Flott laughed as he pulled Gully alongside us. 'You lot are in a wallopy stinksome heap of trouble!'

'It's gone VERY wrong, if you ask me!' snickered Lickspittle. 'You're about to be sluiced!'

The battalion of Queen Latrina's soldiers hauled me, Gully and Morkie into the centre of the square as the cruelsome crowd closed in around us.

'Welcome to the Poodly Plaza!' Grumpwhistle declared. On his command, the guards dropped us to our feet and we gawped around in horror. There was no way we could escape with this many goblins on all sides.

My heart started to race and my knees felt weak as we were marched through the howling horde towards the platform at the far end of the town square. There was a small staircase on one side of the wooden stand, and we were heading straight for it.

'Up you go, you disgusterous bunch of zoolies,' Captain Grumpwhistle sneered. He was really enjoying this, the melon-headed brute! I could tell!

'What do we do, Frankie?' Gully hissed at me with wide frightened eyes as we were pushed up the steps. 'What now?'

'I don't know,' was all I could reply ... and I was telling the truth.

When we reached the top of the platform, I saw a row of huge winches attached to long, rusty cranes. Each one had a metal hook hanging from it on the end of a thick rope, and each hook was dangling above the massive upturned mouth of the open drain. It was the most disgusterous thing I could ever hope to see – or smell.

'I bet you wish you'd stayed in Grimegorn now,

don't you, quarterling?' Grumpwhistle smirked. 'You will very soon!'

'Is that … Is that the …?'

'Poodly-pipe,' the captain finished. 'Yes, it is, boy.'

'And are we …?'

'You're going straight down it,' he jeered through grimy gritted teeth. Then he turned to the cheering crowd and bellowed, 'WHO'S IN THE MOOD FOR A GREAT BIG FLOPSY FLUSHING?'

The mob of goblins went wild. They started throwing vegetables and shrieking.

'THROW 'EM IN HEAD FIRST!'

'Dunk the dunklets!'

'Flush 'em to the dookiest depths!'

I glanced sideways at Gully and Mrs Morkie shaking with terror, and my heart broke. This was all my fault. If it wasn't for me, we'd be safely in our cage back at Grimegorn Safari Park, snoozing or telling stories.

I was just considering throwing myself to my knees and begging for forgiveness, when a commotion in the crowd caught everyone's attention.

'GET OUT OF MY WAY, YOU COMMONLY CANKLES!'

The jostling goblins parted as a gigantic crocodile lumbered towards us with a very irritable-looking Queen Latrina on top.

'MOVE – OR YOU'LL BE SNACKS AND CRUNCHLINGS! DORIS HASN'T HAD HER BREAKFAST!'

CRIME AND PUNISHMENT

'What the blunkers is going on?' the pumpkin-sized ruler snapped. She was wearing a nightgown and tiny hinkapoot slippers, and her bristly hair was knotted round a headful of rollers. 'There had better be a whoppsy good explanation for waking me up from my beauty-tooty sleep … **WELL?'**

'Your Majesty!' Captain Grumpwhistle called from the platform's edge.

'Hmmmm?' The queen looked about in all directions and steered Doris in a full circle, scattering goblins this way and that. 'Who said that?'

'Up here, Your Highness!'

Latrina squinted up at Grumpwhistle and her face creased into a crooked smile.

'Grumpsy! There you are,' she cooed. 'What under the worlds is happening? Are we at war with those skuzzly thistlewumps again? Did we win?'

'Not quite, Your Majesty,' the captain continued. 'You see, these three …'

'BLEEEUUURRRGH!'

The queen heaved a dry retch when she saw what the captain was gesturing to. She looked at us like we'd already been inside the poodly-pipe and had crawled back out. 'You could have warned me, Grumpykins! I nearly pukey-pootled!'

'Sorry, Your Royal Rightness,' Grumpwhistle exclaimed, taking a low bow.

'What the blunkers is that?' Latrina grimaced, pointing at Mrs Morkie. 'It's uglier than my Great-Aunt Repulsa, and she was a total fungus-face!'

'Charming!' Mrs Morkie gasped. 'How rude!'

'This one smells like a bog-bonker's barnyard …' the queen continued, pointing at Gully. 'And that one is …

AAAAAAAAGGGHHHH!!'

No sooner had Queen Latrina laid her piggy little eyes on me, she was squawking and wriggling around in her throne-saddle just like last time.

'It's that horribump HIDEOUS human again!' She yanked on Doris's reins and the hulking creature stomped round in another circle, swiping an entire group of goblins over the edge of the plaza and into the cistern-lake with a dull splash. 'Why is that stinkerish quarterling still here?'

'These cruminals escaped from Grimegorn, Your Majesty,' Captain Grumpwhistle explained as Latrina steered Doris back around to the front.

'WHAT?' The queen glared at us and wrinkled up her squat nose. 'No one escapes from my zoo!'

'WELL, WE DID!' Gully suddenly shouted. He scuffed his hooves and snorted in anger. 'IT WAS EASY!'

Queen Latrina looked so surprised that someone had answered her back, she almost toppled out of her golden seat.

'You're in for it now,' she growled. 'I'll grind the three of you into giblet jam and eat you on crackers!'

'Actually, Your Royal Grumptiousness,' the captain interrupted, pulling a furiously wriggling Viscera Von Tangle from the pouch on his belt and holding her at arm's length. 'There are four.'

Queen Latrina glared at the flailing piskie as though someone was dangling a flea-infested rat in her face, and turned a strange shade of even-greener green. 'Bluh!' she grunted in shock. 'Such repugnuts! I … Um … Guh …'

'Yes, Your Majesty?' the crowd asked. Even from where I was standing on the platform, I could see they were itching for the stumpy queen to hurry up and sentence us.

'Huh-puh!' Latrina heaved in revulsion. 'Bwuh!'

'What is it, Your Majesty?'

'Fluh … Fluh …'

Everyone was holding their breath.

'Fluh … Fluh … **FLUSH THEM DOWN THE POODLY-PIPE! ALL FOUR OF THEM! SPLISH! SPLASH! SPLAT! SPLOO!'**

BRACE YOURSELF!

Okay, my reader friend. We've made it to Chapter 35 and no one has popped their clonkers just yet … but I know what you're thinking.

You're clutching this book with clammy hands, worried and nervous that you're about to turn the page and see me, Gully, Viscera and Mrs Morkie plummet to a poodly end in the dookiest depths of that horrible pipe, aren't you?

Well, don't give up hope just yet. I couldn't be here now, telling you this story, if there hadn't been a whopping great plot twist or two coming up.

So, get ready and brace yourself. It wouldn't be a Frankie Banister story if there wasn't an almighty WHOOOOMF at some point … And while Captain Grumpwhistle and his cronies were stringing us up in the air by our feet from the platform-cranes, we had no idea that the whoooomfiest whoooomf we'd ever heard was about to happen … Even whoooomfier than any of the whoooomfs before.

Here we go …

WHOOOOMF!!!

'It was an honour to know you, my friend,' Gully whimpered as we were lifted high into the air above the dreadful sewer pipe. Those grizzly little goblins had tied us with trap-lace round our ankles and attached the metal hooks to our feet.

Thousands of leering upside-down faces watched as we were winched further and further out over the roaring abyss of sludge and slime.

'Oh, my littl'uns!' Mrs Morkie sobbed. She was so heavy, three cranes had to be used to dangle her in mid-air next to us. 'Just think of picnics and tea … Lots of tea with skunkurrent buns and badger milk biscuits to dunk.'

'Don't say "DUNK!"' Viscera squeaked as she blew about on the end of a tiny thread. 'That's what these grobskwonking goblins are about to do to us!'

While my friends nervously chattered, I couldn't bring myself to say a single word. If I was about to go head first into a gurgling whirlpool of revolting-

smelling sludge, I wanted to be thinking of my family and **The Nothing To See Here Hotel** and all its WONDERFUL inhabitants as I went.

'Prepare to flush the pukelings,' Latrina barked from her throne-saddle.

'NO!' Morkie howled.

'Farewell, my dear friends!' Gully wept.

'This dress cost a fortune!' Viscera screamed.

I clamped my eyes closed. There was a jolt and the sudden thundering of rushing water. I heard the crowds of goblins cheer with glee as we were falling … falli … fa …

Hang on a minute! We weren't moving. I opened my eyes to find that we were still swinging about in exactly the same place over the poodly-pipe and the cheers from the throng of onlookers weren't cheers at all. They were cries of alarm.

'Eh?' Mrs Morkie blurted. 'Is this right?'

Wriggling about to get a better view, I saw that the sound of roaring water was coming from the Great Cistern Lake on the other side of the Poodly Plaza.

The normally calm waters were foaming and churning like they were being boiled and entire fishing boats were being flung into the air by the ferocity of it.

'What's this?' Queen Latrina hollered, steering Doris round to face the surging lake. 'Who is interrupting my flush-tivities?! I demand to know what's going—

WHOOOOOOOOOOOOOOOOOOMMMMFFFFFF!!!

There was an explosion of water, followed by a great fizzing sound, as a colossal bubble rose into view from the dark depths. It shimmered and sparkled in the mushroom-light like a Drooltide bauble … and there, inside its delicate walls, was a spectacular PIRATE GALLEON!

It was all happening so fast, I could hardly keep up.

The bubble popped, with an ear-splitting PING that echoed off the vast cistern walls, and I got a clearer view of the ship inside it. Even though I was upside-down and feeling very woozy, something about the many people rushing about on the galleon's deck seemed vaguely familiar. Like a memory from long ago …

It wasn't until a short, tattooed figure with ratty dreadlocks clambered onto the ship's railing, brandished a cutlass and yelled,

'GIVE ME BACK MY FRANKIE, YOU BUNCH OF SQUITLERS! WHERE'S THE BOY?'

that I realised who I was looking at.

'Maudlin?!' I cried, feeling like my heart might topple out of my mouth and vanish down the poodly-pipe. My leprechaun friend was here in Gradibash and she was standing on the bow of … of … **THE *BLISTERED BARNACLE*! CALAMITUS PLANK'S SHIP!** I hadn't seen it since it had smashed through the hotel's foyer and Captain Plank, the most famous goblin pirate of them all, retrieved his magical diamond dentures from thieving little Grogbah. 'MAUDLIN, we're up here!!'

Now, I'll do my best to explain everything that happened next, but there was so much chaos and I was SO confused, it wasn't too easy to take it all in.

In seconds, there was a wild howl as several of Captain Plank's crew of Squall Goblins swung on ropes from the tall masts of the ship and landed amongst the poshly crowds jostling about in the plaza.

These seafaring rumpscallions were much taller than the squat inhabitants of Gradibash and they barged their way through the startled crowds, swinging cutlasses and firing pistols.

'Move, you bulging bunch of blighters!' a familiar voice shouted as its owner reached the bottom of the wooden steps and climbed into view.

From where I was dangling, I watched a pair of buckle-covered boots stomp their way across the platform.

'What have you got yourself into, Frankie Banister?' The voice spoke again. I lifted my eyes past the buckled boots, past a peacock blue coat.

'TEMPESTRA!' I cheered.

I swear, I don't think I've ever been so pleased to see a goblin in all my life. It was Calamitus's daughter and second in command on the **BLISTERED BARNACLE,** Tempestra Plank. She stormed her way across the wonky boards and ordered the nearest worker, who was controlling my crane, to reel me back in.

'Do it now, or I'll personally throw you down that pipe myself,' she commanded, swishing her cutlass this way and that.

In no time, I was lowered onto the platform and the trap-lace around my ankles had been cut loose.

Tempestra offered me a hand and pulled me to my wobbly feet.

'Good to see you, Frankie,' she said with a mischievous grin. 'And not a moment too soon, it seems.'

'Tempestra! I didn't think I'd ever see you again!'

'You honestly thought you'd seen the last of me?' she laughed. 'Dunglebrain!'

'But how did you know where to look?' I asked,

giddy with relief. 'I've been gone for—'

'Three weeks, two days and seven hours,' Tempestra interrupted. 'Your mum and dad were in a right snivelicious worry-rumpus.'

'Erm, I say, deary,' Mrs Morkie stammered behind me. 'I don't suppose you can get us down too, could you? I can barely feel my footsies.'

'Who are they?' asked Tempestra. She glanced over my shoulder at the three other dangling figures.

'These are my friends,' I replied. 'We were prisoners together. They have to come too!'

'Aye aye,' Tempestra nodded, and she busied herself marching along the row of cranes, ordering each one to be lowered with her sword raised above her head.

'Oh, it's a pleasure to meet you.' Mrs Morkie smiled a nervous smile and did a little curtsy, after she'd flopped onto the platform with a *BUMP* and clambered to her feet. 'Any friend of Frankie is a friend of mine, my scrumplet.'

'I can't thank you enough,' Gully joined in. He was holding Viscera in his hand and carefully helped her into his waistcoat pocket.

'Are we all present and correct?' Tempestra asked.

'AYE AYE!' we chorused back.

'**AVAST!**' she barked, grabbing a pistol from her belt and firing it into the air for extra flare and fanciness. 'To the **BLISTERED BARNACLE!**'

I turned round to the staircase that led down from the platform and stopped.

In all the craziness, we'd failed to notice Queen Latrina skulking towards us on top of her gigantic crocodile. Now the terrible creature was waiting at the bottom of the steps, its jagged jaws wide open.

'Going somewhere, sea scumlies?' Latrina broke the silence. She had the look of someone who'd just swallowed a wasps' nest. 'Have my brains been swizzled? Have my peepers gone potty? Who the blunkers are you rottly lot and what exactly do you think you're doing with my flushables?'

Tempestra sidled to the edge of the platform and glowered down at the pumpkin-sized ruler.

'I AM TEMPESTRA PLANK, DAUGHTER OF CALAMITUS PLANK, THE FIEND OF THE SEVEN SEWERS, AND WE HAVE COME TO FREE YOUR PRISONER.'

'Prisoners!' I whispered in the goblin girl's ear. 'Free all the prisoners.'

'And we have come to free ALL your prisoners, you hideous old humpler!'

'HUMPLER!' Queen Latrina gasped in horror. 'You've made a honkly big mistake, Miss **PLONK!** No one leaves Gradibash unless I say so.'

'Let us leave quietly and we'll have no reason to boot you in the bumly-bits,' Tempestra said calmly.

'NOT ON YOUR NELLY!' Latrina scoffed. 'Your skuzzly feet are going nowhere near the royal rump, make no mistakings!' She looked at the few members of pirate crew who'd swung ashore with

Tempestra and laughed at them, then pointed down at the crocodile beneath her as if they'd failed to spot it. 'Allow me to introduce you to Doris. She eats bilge-rumples like you lot for breakfast!'

'That's funny,' Tempestra replied. 'We eat crocodile nuggets for breakfast aboard the **BLISTERED BARNACLE.** Every morning! They're delicious.'

The queen laughed sarcastically, but it didn't take an expert to see the twitch of nervousness on her grotsome face.

'You might be all tallish and flashy with your swords and pistols and crocodile nuggets,' Latrina sneered. 'but you're no match for my goblin guards.'

'Maybe not,' Tempestra replied. 'But they are!'

She pointed back at the galleon and a bonejangling roar went up around the city. While Latrina had been distracted by us on the poodly-platform, the **BLISTERED BARNACLE** had moored right up against the plaza walls, and all of Captain Plank's crew had gathered on deck. They were a fearsome bunch, poised and ready for battle. There were hordes of pirates, hollering and cursing, and amongst them I spotted …

A great sob blurted uncontrollably out of my mouth.

Mum and Dad were standing with Maudlin. Nancy was halfway up the mast with cutlasses in all four of her hands, Ooof was brandishing a mop and a broom from the hotel cloakroom, and the Molar Sisters were ready with their wands. Even Granny Regurgita was here!!

'Frankie, my darling!' Mum yelled. I could barely hear her across the fussing crowd. 'We love you!'

'You're so brave, son,' Dad joined in. 'You're a hero!'

Before I could shout back to them, there was a strange grunt from below us.

'**BLUH!**' It was Queen Latrina. 'Are those … are those more … are those more **HUMANS?**'

In a flash, pandemonium broke out across the Poodly Plaza as the queen let rip a scream that could have shattered an iceberg. She yanked on Doris's reins and the giant reptile bulldozed through the crowd, sending courtiers and civilians flying through the air like squat overdressed ping-pong balls.

'*DON'T LET HER GET AWAY!*' a deep and gravelly voiced boomed from the ship. I looked up and saw that Calamitus Plank himself was standing in the crow's nest at the very top of the tallest mast, shouting through a rusty loudhailer.

'GRAB 'EM, ME HONKERS! SHOW THOSE LAND-LUMPERS NOT TO MESS WITH THE LIKES OF US SALTY SEA DONKS!'

With that, Captain Plank leaped down and his pirate crew came pouring across the gangplank or swung to shore on sail ropes. They teemed onto the plaza and started chasing the queen's guards in all directions.

I watched with the greatest feeling of happiness and joy as Nancy catapulted herself off the main mast and right into the middle of the action on two lengths of web, while Mum, Dad and Maudlin ran ashore, making their way towards me as they batted petrified Barrow Goblins aside.

'GO!' Tempestra barked. 'Find your family. I'll protect your friends.'

I didn't need to be told twice. Completely forgetting about any danger, I leaped down the steps two and three at a time, then sprinted across the cobbled square, dodging brawling pirates and hurdling royal guards as I went.

'MUM!' I shouted so loudly I thought my head might explode. **'DAD!!'**

I skidded past Officer Flott as he was hit by a blast of tooth-fairy magic. The Molar Sisters were dancing in a circle, singing and swatting their wonky wands above their heads, conjuring little tornados. Flott was snatched off the ground and spun through the air like a furious frisbee.

'Fantathtic!' the triplets cooed in unison, twirling about and grinning gappy grins. 'It'th tho lovely to thee you, Frankie!'

I bounded past Ooof as he was attempting to fight with Officer Lickspittle. The little goblin kept jabbing him in the knees with her tiny sword, but it was like poking a rhinoceros with matchsticks.

'Ow! Hello, Frankie! Ow!' Ooof waved one of his tree-trunk arms and accidentally thwacked Lickspittle into a pile of stinking fishing nets that were drying in a corner. 'Ooof miss you, Frankie!'

'I missed you too!' I shouted over my shoulder as I darted round our handyogre, ducking just in time to avoid his flailing fists.

And then … there they were. Maudlin Maloney was slightly ahead of Mum and Dad, and she flung her gnarled hands round my waist, holding on tight.

'Oh, you brainboogled wee eejit!' she snivelled into my tummy as she squeezed me harder and harder. 'My heart's been hobbled! What did you have to go and do a thing like getting snitched for?'

A large teardrop rolled down my cheek. I couldn't help it. I knew the ancient old leprechaun had just been in a bad mood back at the hotel and she loved me really.

'I've been worried sickly, I have. The girls have all been blurty and haven't B-KAWKED once while you've been away!'

As if on cue, Maudlin's chickens appeared through the chaos and clucked around my feet. B-KAWK!

'Oh, would you listen to that!' the old leprechaun wept. 'I haven't seen Eggwina this happy in weeks! Henelope's laid an egg with joy, look!'

'Frankie!' Mum and Dad caught up with Maudlin and threw their arms round both of us.

'Oh, my beautiful boy!' Mum blubbed. 'My beautiful boy!'

'You're a sight for salty eyes!' Dad sniffled, wiping his tears with the end of his tail. 'Let me look at you!'

We could have stood there hugging all day if there hadn't been a raging goblin battle thundering around us.

'It was Grogbah who had me kidnapped!' I suddenly yelled as I came to my senses. 'His mangy mother put me in a zoo!'

'What?' Maudlin gasped. 'That skuzzling skrunt!'

'There are still hundreds of creatures locked up in there,' I continued. 'We can't leave them!'

Just then Granny Regurgita hurtled through the crowd like a raging bull. She was clutching the goblin maiden with a face like a dropped omelette by the back of her frilly dress and she swung the wretched thing through the air and into an oncoming squadron of soldiers like it was a game of skittles.

'Oh, it's you …' she growled when she finally glanced down and spotted me. 'Look at the mess you've caused, boy.'

'It wasn't my fault!'

'I said we should just leave you to your new life as a goblin – it'd serve you right – but your mother was all squisherous and wanted to save you.'

'It's nice to see you too, Granny,' I said. Believe it or not, that's one of the nicest things she's ever said to me.

'So, what now?' Dad shouted over the din. 'Shall we get out of here?'

'Not yet, Bargeous!' Maudlin said. 'We need to teach that quarrelish queen and her simpering son a thing or two.'

'You mean we can finally grunch Grogbog?' I asked.

'When I get these scabberous hands on that little

lumper, I'll whomp him back to next Wungleswatch, the spineless spook! And his mother! Where'd she go?'

I looked at the path of destruction left by Doris as she galumphed through the crowd and saw that it led straight to the doors of the palace. That lily-livered conk of a queen had scarpered off to hide!

'The queen will be in there!' I yelled, pointing to the glass building. 'So will Grogbah.'

'Righty, then,' Granny Regurgita grunted. 'Let's go.'

· 37 ·

TAKE THAT!

We fought our way through the clamouring goblins as quickly as we could, heading for Queen Latrina's palace.

'You rambunking wee jobby!' I heard a voice yell ahead of me. 'Maybe next time you'll think twice before signing up to be a crone's cronie!'

It was Nancy! I didn't care that she was in the middle of fighting a gaggle of royal guards, so

I shoved right past them all and hurled myself into her giant spider arms.

'No, you don't!' she yelped as I grabbed hold of her. 'You're not too quick for this Orkney Brittle-Back!'

Before I could stop her, Nancy grabbed me by the ankle and was about to fling me into the lake, thinking I was another attacking soldier.

'Nancy, it's me!' I yelped as loudly as I could over the deafening roar of the battle. 'Frankie!'

'Oh, my wee lamb!' Nancy shrieked when she realised who she was clutching in her hands. 'I was about to toss you away!'

I looked up at Nancy and she beamed down at me.

'My heart could burst, so it could! We've all been worried sick, Frankie.'

'I missed you so much,' I said as another tear ran down my face.

'We missed you t— OW!' We both looked down to see a particularly young Barrow Goblin whacking away at Nancy's back legs with a rusty spoon.

'One moment, petal.' Nancy smiled, batting her eight eyelids at me. Then she reached down and picked the stumpy goblin up by the scruff of his collar.

'I'm not sure you want to be doing that,' she said to the wriggling goblin. 'Does your moomsie know you're out?'

The goblin shook his head.

'Have you noticed there are bloodthirsty pirates running about the place?'

The goblin nodded.

'Run off home, poppet.' Nancy placed the goblin back on the ground and patted him on the back. 'Be safe!'

'Where were we?' I laughed, as I watched the goblin child scarper in the direction of the town. I was just about to explain to Nancy all about what had happened, when a shrill and extremely loud voice echoed all around the Great Cistern City.

'Shut your mumble-holes! All of you!'

I looked up and saw that Queen Latrina was standing on the top tower of her palace, and she'd produced an even bigger and more battered megaphone than Calamitus.

The entire crowd went silent as Barrow and Squall Goblins alike all turned to see what was going on.

'As Your Royal Grumptiousness, Ruler of the Rabble and Godly of Goodliness, I want to tell you all that I'm very bored! Unless we're winning … Are we winning?'

Hundreds of Latrina's royal guards all shook their heads in unison.

'Then I'm very bored!'

Nobody said a word.

'Everyone knows that I'm supposed to be the winner at everything, I'm the queen, and when I don't get my own way I get very cross and squitly.'

Still nobody spoke.

'With that in mind, I demand all of you prattly pirate-types to bog off back to where you came from. You're different from us Barrow Goblins and that's disgusterous!'

All the Barrow Goblins in the throng cheered and whooped at this.

'And ... I'm also feeling very stroply at my own courtiers and every peasanty pook who lives in Gradibash. You're all complete commonly skuzzlers and I want new subjects. Better, more worshipful ones! So, I command you to form an orderly line and jump into the poodly-pipe. Off you go!'

There was a long moment of confused silence and then, to my astonishment, all the Barrow Goblins of Gradibash started milling their way over to form a long queue at the base of the wooden platform. They were actually going to line up, and one by one, hop into the gurgling grossness of the poodly-pipe!

'No, wait! This isn't how it should end!' I yelled, but my voice wasn't loud enough for everybody to hear across the plaza.

'You don't have to do this!'

It was no use. The Barrow Goblins were already mumbling their goodbyes and not listening. How were we going to stop them? I couldn't stand there fussing while the innocent citizens of Gradibash jumped to their poodly peril just because Latrina told them to!

'Here, boy!' Maudlin pushed her way towards me and Nancy. She reached into one of the many pouches on her belt and pulled out what looked like a tiny green snail shell. 'Eat this!'

'Eurgh, why?' I asked.

'It's the shell of a shrillig, it'll make your voice ten times louder! DO IT!'

I placed the small thing on the end of my tongue and crunched it between my teeth, grimacing. It tasted like smelly feet and sour pondwater.

'Go on, then, Frankie,' Maudlin encouraged me as Nancy held me up as high as she could. 'Quick or they'll all be poppin' their clonkers before you know it!'

'Hello?' I said, and my voice thundered across the crowd like a giant's.

Everyone jumped with surprise and I watched as they all turned to stare at me.

'You don't need to leap into the poodly-pipe because that ranciderous rumplet told you to!' I bellowed.

'But she's our queen ...' a sickly-looking goblin whimpered.

'SO WHAT?' I said.

'Don't listen to him, you dirty bunch of snotlings,' Queen Latrina announced. 'I want all of you in that pipe – right now! I need to make room for my adoring new subjects, so you've got to hop it!'

All the Barrow Goblins turned to go again. This was MADNESS!!!

'STOP!' I yelled, and the entire city shook. **'You don't have to listen to her or Grogbah, if you don't want to!'**

'The boy is right!' Calamitus called from the top of the ship's mast.

'NONKUMBUMPS!'

Latrina screamed. **'You be quiet, you dusty bag-o-bones. My voice-trumpety-thingumy-bob is much bigger than yours.'**

Calamitus opened his diamond-dentures to shout back, then suddenly looked extremely lost for words and shrugged down at me, Nancy and Maudlin with a muddled expression. Having an empty skull for a head meant witty retorts weren't his greatest talent, I guess.

'Now, I won't say it again,' Latrina growled, turning back round to glare at the crowds of upturned faces. **'Take no notice of that bonejangled bungler and GET IN THE PIPE!'**

And that's when things got interesting …

'No!' a single tiny voice called from the throng.

For a moment, we all remained in confused silence. Had we really just heard that? Were our ears playing tricks?

'No!' came another voice, and another, and another. 'No! No! NOOOO!'

Queen Latrina's jaw flapped wide open and her piggy little eyes nearly bulged out of her face.

'What did you just say?' she sneered. 'Are you all boogled in the bonce?'

'I don't want to jump in the poodly-pipe!' a goblin guard cried, puffing out his chest.

'Me neither!' called one of the royal handmaidens. 'I'm not in a poodly mood!'

'Mu ... Mu ... MUTINY MONGERS!' Latrina hollered at her people. 'Fine! Ignore my orders! Don't flush yourselves away, you bundle of belchers. You can all stay right here where it's nice and dry.'

'Do ... Do you mean it?' I stammered in my booming voice. Maybe the queen wasn't such a massive gonker after all? 'Are you surrendering?'

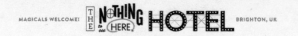

'NOT ON YOUR NELLY!' Latrina squawked back at me, before shifting her loudspeaker down towards the palace doors. **'DORIS! GET OUT HERE!'**

38

A LITTLE MORE REVENGE

A petrified gasp rippled through the mass of chattering goblins.

Everyone turned and stared with trembling knees as the green-glass doors of the palace crept silently open, revealing the queen's monstrous pet.

'Ah, there you are, Doris-i-kins!' Latrina cooed down from her perch on the tower. 'You're going to have a very special breakfast today, my bumpsome beauty.'

We all held our breath as the dreadful reptile began stalking its way through the high arch, swinging its gargantuan head to glare in our direction.

'Gulp 'em all!' Latrina chuckled spitefully. 'Every last one!'

This was it. We had no hope against a thing like Doris. With one quick bound, she would clamp her mighty jaws round me and Maudlin at the same time before we'd had chance to scream.

'Don't even think about it, you overgrown iguana,' Maloney growled, taking a few defiant steps towards the crocodile as it emitted a rumble from deep in its belly. 'I want to have a word with you.'

'Maudlin!' I whispered at the back of the ancient leprechaun's head. 'What are you doing?'

'Hush!' she hissed at me over my shoulder. 'We didn't come this far to be a lizard's lunch.'

With that, Maudlin started wriggling on the

spot and grunting out a strange guttural noise. It sounded like the time she ate a dragon chilli at dinner and couldn't speak for hours afterwards.

'Guh-wah!' Maudlin snorted. 'Gub-ruh! Muh! Gwah!'

'What are you saying to my crocodarling, witch?' Latrina scoffed at Maloney. 'Doris, eat her first!'

'Brooah-gah!' Maudlin continued, jiggling about on the spot. It seemed as if the gigantic crocodile was completely transfixed by her bizarre performance. 'Bluh! Guh! Woah!'

'DORIS, ARE YOU LISTENING TO MOOMSIE?'

After a few more grumbles and wobbles, Maloney finished whatever she was up to, patted down her crinkled clothes and turned back to face me.

'There,' she said with a wonky grin. 'That should do the trick.'

'GET THEM, DORIS!'

Latrina yowled, aiming her loudspeaker right at the giant beast. 'Grunch their bones and crunch their crumpets!'

There was the teensiest of terrifying moments when I thought the scaly monster might do as she was ordered.

'DO IT, DORIS!' Latrina squawked again. **'I'M YOUR QUEEN AND I COMMAND YOU TO—'**

Before Latrina could shout another word, the crocodile thundered away from us and flopped over the side of the Just-About-In-The-Middle-Bridge, vanishing into the murky waters below.

'Doris?' Latrina grunted into her megaphone. **'DORIS!!'**

'Haha! You swizzled eejit!' Maloney cackled up at the pumpkin-sized queen. 'Even your reptile can't stand you!'

'What did you say to her, you leather-faced loon?'

'I told Doris about a lovely wee spot I know in a cistern far away from this muck-dump. Plenty of sewer slugs and fishes galore. It's a watery wonderland, so it is, and there's not a single gormerous goblin to be found.'

'YOU ROTTLERS!' Latrina's bulbous

face was starting to turn purple with rage. She gripped hold of the ornate glass railing on the tower balcony and snarled down at us.

'Now what are you going to do, Princess Plop?' Maudlin cackled with glee.

'I'M GOING TO TEAR YOU INTO LEPRECHAUN-FETTI!' Queen Latrina screeched, squeezing the rail tighter and tighter with anger. **'I'LL PUNCH YOU ALL IN THE POMPLES! I'LL DOOF YOU IN THE DINGLES! I'M THE QUEEN AND I ALWAYS WI—**

AAAAAAAAAAAAAAAAAAAAGGGHH!'

Before Latrina had even realised what she'd done, the railing clenched between her tiny hands shattered and she toppled forwards, falling straight over the edge of the tower balcony like a plummeting pumpkin.

'Catch her, Nancy!' Maudlin barked.

'Right you are, deary!' She was still holding me in two of her hands, but with the spare pair, Nancy quickly snatched the shrieking queen before she hit the ground.

'YOU CRUMINALS!' Latrina squealed as she found herself dangling upside down by her pudgy ankle, kicking her free leg about like a baby having a tantrum. **'YOU SKUZZLERS!'**

'A thank you might be nice,' said Nancy, lifting Latrina up to her eye level and shaking her head disapprovingly. 'Naughty little whelpling.'

'GET OFF ME!' the furious goblin shouted.

It was difficult not to laugh as Nancy turned the queen the right way up and placed her gently down on the cobbles. She looked like she'd been dragged through a thistle patch backwards.

'Right! Now you're all going to pay!' Latrina spat. She was so hopping mad, I thought she might actually start … well … hopping.

'GRUMPWHISTLE!' she shrieked. 'Where are you? Arrest these rumpskallions at once!'

A groan rose up behind us and the shocked-faced crowd of goblins parted to reveal a blobby … a gloopy … for a second I wasn't sure what I was looking at until it opened its mouth and I realised that Grumpwhistle had lost a scuffle with the Molar Sisters. His once beautiful blood-red armour had been changed into toothpaste that slopped down his front and dripped off his legs in mint-scented globs.

'Ah, Grumpsy!' Latrina cooed, when she spotted him. 'Sort out this mess for me, Grumpkins. Arrest these gurnips and find me a new croco-daughter. There's a dunkling.'

Captain Grumpwhistle raised himself up to his full height, lifted his arm as if to salute his queen, and then … scooped a huge fistful of toothpaste from where his helmet used to sit on his head and lobbed it at her.

'**I QUIT!**' he humphed as the splat of stripy slime hit Latrina right in the face. 'You can do your own dirty work from now on!'

Before Latrina could utter a word, Grumpwhistle turned on his heels and trudged off through the city, sulking to himself.

Every face in the Poodly Plaza stared at Queen Latrina. She looked like the tiniest and most miserable volcano in the world, that might just explode at any moment.

'Now you've lost your people, your beast and your royal guards, you rancid old foozle-fart,' Maudlin spluttered, trying to stop herself from bursting into hysterical giggles. 'I bet you wish you'd been a bit nicer now, eh?'

'Shut your goblet!' Latrina barked. 'I'm still the queen!'

'A QUEEN WITH NO SUBJECTS!' a voice shouted from somewhere in the huge crush of goblins.

'Bog off!' yelled another. 'Cantunkerous old windbag!'

'I never liked you!'

'You were a rubbish queen!'

'I heard the Bermuda Triangle is nice this time of year.'

'We're leaving!'

'Yeah, let's get out of this 'orrible place.'

Before long, every goblin in Gradibash was hurrying off to pack up their homes, nattering about where they'd like to go and what they'd like to see.

'Well, that's that,' Granny Regurgita croaked as she wandered over to join the few of us left in front of the palace. 'You're on your own, Your Majesty.'

'Good!' Latrina whined back at Granny. She folded her arms across her belly and pouted her crusty lips. 'Just how I want it! No one is good enough company for me, anyway. I'm glad I'll be on my own. There will be more snacklies for me and no one else. I don't want to look at another fuzzly face ever again.'

'Fine,' Granny Regurgita grumbled. 'I think it's time to lea—'

There was a small and sudden explosion of ectoplasm above her and – you guessed it again – Grogbah appeared.

'MOOMSIE!' he trilled, waving his arms and legs about like a carbuncled Catherine wheel. 'Don't forget me! I'll be here to keep you company!'

Latrina grimaced up at Grogbah and stuck out her tongue.

'Oh no you won't!' she said, puffing out her cheeks. 'You're haunting that rotsy Franky-thing and he's going straight back to where he came from. You've got to go too. Them's the rules!'

'No, Moomsie! I want to stay with you. We can live in royal rapture, just the two of us. Think of the lovely chattywags we'll have.'

'You ain't staying here, you dim-twitted donker!'

'But, Moomsie, PLEASE!'

I watched as Maloney stepped closer to the squabbling goblins, then reached into the knots of her dreadlocks and pulled out a thin wand made from unicorn horn.

'I think this can be arranged,' Maudlin tittered, before drawing a few invisible runes in the air with the little object.

'What are you up to, you tricksy old turnip?' Latrina gawped as delicate specks of light suddenly twinkled in a wavering line between me and Grogbah. I felt a strange tingling sensation all over my skin. And then ... it was gone.

'I've broken the haunting,' Maudlin said. 'You're no longer attached to Frankie, Grogbog.'

'I'M NOT!?!' Grogbah looked like he was going to belch ectoplasm everywhere with happiness. 'I don't have to stick around with you mucklies any more?'

'Ah, that's better, isn't it?' Latrina beamed, smiling a fake smile. 'Now you're free to go anywhere you want, son. Anywhere as far away from here as possible. Antarctica's nice! Why not the moon?'

'Not so fast,' Maudlin chuckled, raising the wand again.

'NO!' Latrina yelped, guessing what Maloney was about to do. **'Don't even think about it, you rambunking rottler!'** But it was too late. Maudlin swished the wand a second time and a new line of twinkling lights briefly appeared between the queen and her spook-son.

'Consider yourself haunted, Your Majesty. Think of it as a parting gift from Manky Old Maloney,' the ancient leprechaun cackled. 'Grogbah, you've got a new person to pester, and I made sure it's a very short leash!'

'MOOMSIE!' Grogbah wailed in delight. **'IT'S YOU AND ME FOR EVER!'**

AND THAT WAS THAT ...

So, there you have it, my reader friend.

The last we saw of Queen Latrina, she was screaming like a banshee and sprinting back into the palace, with her joyfully singing son being dragged along behind her by an invisible thread. Haha!

By the time we'd all regrouped in the Poodly Plaza, the pirates had started to board the ship again. Calamitus had shimmied back down from the crow's nest and was barking orders to his crew, preparing to set sail on the voyage back to **The Nothing To See Here Hotel**. I smiled at the rattling skeleton when we spotted each other and he made straight for me.

'Avast, Frankie!' Calamitus wheezed, patting a

bony hand on my back. 'I think there's the makings of a ruddy good sea donk in you, m'boy. It seems you've got buccaneer blood in your veins. Want to come sail with old Captain Plank in the seven sewers?'

'**NO!**' Dad snapped when he heard Calamitus's offer from a little way off.

'Absolutely no more adventures,' Mum agreed. 'Never again!'

'Suit your selflies,' the skeleton chuckled. He winked at me and staggered off to do more captain-ish things.

In no time there was excited activity everywhere.

Tempestra led a gaggle of her best crew up to Grimegorn to open all the cages and set Latrina's magical menagerie free, and I was thrilled to see that Gully and Mrs Morkie had arrived safely on board. It made me SO HAPPY to introduce my new friends to Mum, Dad, Nancy and Maudlin and invite them to come stay at the hotel for good.

D'you know, it turns out that Limpet Lil, the wooden welcome wench at the Itchy Urchin, was the whole reason I was rescued at all! Who'd have thought?

I couldn't believe it when Mum told me.

That BRILLIANT mulchy maiden got a grumbly worried feeling after we met on the night of my kidnapping, and she decided to write and tell her cousin all about it.

Just by luck, Lil's cousin is Grizzled Gracy-Lou, the skeleton figurehead of the *BLISTERED BARNACLE*! It took yonks and yonkers for the news to reach her because wooden wenches like Lil only use the hermit-crab postal service. They're extremely reliable, those little crustaceans, but they're about as slow as a post-creature can get!

Anyway, where was I?

Oh, yes! Once everyone was back on the ship, the streets of Gradibash were running alive with curious exotic animals, and we'd figured out a way of putting Morkie towards the back of the deck while we all headed to the front to keep it balanced, we were ready to weigh anchor.

That would probably have been the end of this story if …

'WAIT!' I cried. **'DON'T SET SAIL!'**

Maudlin was preparing to cast the bubble charm when I spotted a tall cloaked figure slipping into an alleyway just across the plaza.

'Impya!' I shouted. Before I had time to think, I bounded down the gangplank. **'Impya!'**

I could hear my parents and Nancy calling behind me, but there was no way I was going to leave this place without saying thank you to the strange frog-woman. Without her help, we'd still be locked inside Grimegorn.

'Wait!'

The alleyway was a tiny passage of cobblestones that ran behind the Poodly Plaza called Slug-slither Lane. When I reached it, I could already see Impya was almost at the far end, but I know she had heard me yelling.

'Impya, it's me!'

The frog-lady stopped in her tracks.

'What is it, boy?' she said over her shoulder.

'Everyone is leaving Gradibash! You don't need to hide in the shadows any more. The guards have fled and no one will throw stones or be cruel.'

'So?'

'So … You should leave too. You don't have to wander the pipes alone. Come and meet my family.'

'Don't talk such judderish,' Impya replied. She turned to look at me and I could see sadness in her eyes. 'No one wants to spend time with the Slime Wife.'

'Come back to **The Nothing To See Here Hotel** with us. We're all weird and wonderful there,' I said. 'You'd love my great-great-great-grandad Abraham. He was an explorer too, remember? Sort of like you.'

Impya took a single step closer to me.

'Grandad Abe tells stories much better than I do,' I continued, trying to encourage her. 'He could tell you all about the world above, and things to see, and all those stories about Oculus Nocturne. I bet you'd love those!'

The frog-lady padded out of the shadows on her long feet.

'Oculus Nocturne,' she sighed.

'Yes!' If I wasn't mistaken, it looked like I was getting through to her. 'Grandad Abe can tell you the stories about Oculus far better than I can. They're completely BONKERS!'

Impya walked closer and stopped just in front of me, then bent down until her face was very close to mine.

'All right,' she whispered. 'All right.'

·40·

ONE LAST TWIST

I don't think I'll ever feel something more belly-bungling and humdifferous than the moment we arrived back at the hotel. I could have stood for hours in the front doorway, taking in all the familiar clatter and noise and smells and colours and music and light of the place.

My heart nearly flew straight out of my chest when Hoggit came bounding from the kitchens and leaped into my arms, puffing out a tiny chain of smoke rings.

I'm not too proud to admit to you, my reader friend, that I had a blunking good cry at that moment.

'So, this is your amazing home,' Gully said, putting his hand on my shoulder and giving me a slightly soggy smile. 'I can see why you missed it.'

After a very damp and gloomy journey back to the surface in the **BLISTERED BARNACLE**'s enchanted bubble, we were all shivering and huddling together in the foyer trying to keep warm. Mum and Dad handed out blankets and Nancy poured mug after mug of shrimp-scale tea. Mrs Morkie was delighted. HAHA!

But don't worry. I'm not going to end this story talking about mugs of hot drinks, I promise.

This chapter wouldn't be called 'One Last Twist' if there wasn't one last twist. So, here it is.

After we'd had our tea, I showed Gully, Morkie and Impya around the hotel. Well, Morkie only saw the bits she could squeeze into, but she didn't mind. We'd just been up to the observatorium and Impya had taken a cooling dip in the mud spa, when I mentioned I wanted her to meet Grandad Abe.

At first, she seemed quite curious, but when we got to the bottom of the great staircase and she spotted his ghost floating near Aunt Zennifer's fountain, the frog-lady got very nervous and twitchy.

'Are you all right?' I asked her. 'Don't worry, he's super friendly.'

'I can't, Frankie,' she mumbled, visibly shaking.

'Of course you can!'

'No, a great explorer like Abraham Banister wouldn't be interested in a wandering Slime Wife. I shouldn't have come.'

She turned to go towards the front door, but I grabbed her by the wrist.

'You must stay,' I pleaded. 'You saved our lives back in Grimegorn. You're my friend.'

Impya stared at me with her large orange eyes, and a smile crept across her face.

'You're a very kind person, Frankie Banister. I

shan't forget that, but I must get away from here. I don't belong.'

'You can be part of our family, Impya!' I said, feeling a little hurt. 'I thought you wanted to live with us,'

'So did I,' she whispered. 'But I was wrong. There are things I have to do.'

With that, Impya plucked a trinket from her cloak and pressed it into my hand.

'It's a little something to remember me by, but don't look until I'm gone.'

She turned and hurried across the foyer.

I was just thinking about running after her when Mum and Dad returned from gathering more blankets and they bounded over to see me.

'There you are.' Mum beamed, planting a slobberchopsy kiss on my head and draping a blanket round my shoulders. 'You're right back where you belong, my darling.'

'Yep,' I said, hardly listening. I couldn't see where Impya had gone, and something in my gut told me I should try again to make her stay.

'Are you okay?' Dad asked, when he saw me frowning. 'Frankie, what is it?'

'The frog-lady,' I said.

'The one who came back on the ship with us?' Mum asked, pulling a face. 'I didn't like her. She gave me goosebumps. So slimy!'

'She's lonely,' I replied. 'But she said she didn't belong here.'

It was right at that moment I opened my fingers and glanced absent-mindedly down at the delicate silver brooch that she'd pressed into my palm.

I opened my mouth to speak, but nothing came out. The hairs on the back of my neck prickled and my skin turned to goosebumps.

'Frankie?' Mum asked as she saw my face turn pale. 'Frankie, you've gone as white as a spook, you're frightening me.'

There, in the palm of my hand, was a piece of jewellery I'd looked at hundreds of times before. Set in the shape of the letters O and N, I recognised it the second I saw it. It belonged to my great-great-uncle's mother, Olympia Nocturne.

'IT'S HER!'

I yelled.

Suddenly her name made perfect sense. Why hadn't I noticed before? Impya is just a shortened version of Olympia!!

Hearing me yelp, Grandad Abe floated over, beaming from ear to ear.

'Frankie, my boy! It's splundish to have you back!' he chuckled. 'You gave us a real fright when you vanished.'

'I'm about to give you another one,' I stammered to the friendly phantom.

'Oh?' Abraham's fuzzy eyebrows gathered into a frown. 'Go on.'

'What's all this about?' Dad asked.

'Grandad, when you and your first family stumbled upon the graveghast all those years ago, what happened to your wife, Olympia? Remind me …'

'Oh, well, according to the photograph that accidentally caught the whole rotten affair, she was turned into a  toad. Yes, that's right. A big old hoppity-toad.'

'I don't think that's quite right,' I said with a

trembling voice. I felt like my knees might give way beneath me. 'She was turned into something much stranger.'

'What do you mean?' Mum snapped. I could tell she was growing impatient.

'The frog-lady – she's **OLYMPIA NOCTURNE!!**'

'Oh my goodness!' Mum gasped. 'Are you sure?'

'Where did she go?' Dad huffed as he frantically started searching about.

'OLYMPIA'S HERE?' Grandad Abe started flapping about in mid-air. No one tell Regurgita! She'll go completely gruzzly!'

'Oh, blunkers!' Maudlin barked, listening from a little way off. 'We have to stop her!'

'There! Look!' Mum said, pointing at a trail of slime that led across the foyer floor and into the library.

'Oh no!' My brain started to race ahead of me and I knew what had happened before I even made it to the door. Back in Grimegorn, I'd told Impya EVERYTHING about Oculus. I'd even jabbered on about where his body was imprisoned in a block of ice, and … 'SHE KNOWS OCULUS'S SPECTRIL IS IN THE LIBRARY! SHE'S GOING TO TRY AND RESCUE HIM!'

Dad and I raced ahead of everyone else, with Mum and the rest of our little group bounding along behind.

As I reached the archway over the library entrance, I slipped in the slime trail and careered across the floor, hitting my head and my back with a painful thump.

'It's gone!' Dad wheezed. 'IT'S GONE, FRANKIE! She's taken the jar!'

I looked up to where he was pointing and saw that the shelves of the tallest bookcase were all dripping in mucus, and the top one that had stored Oculus's spectril was now empty.

'She can't have gone far,' I said, scrabbling back to my feet. But as I did I noticed the library window was wide open and the curtains were flapping in the cold winter air. Olympia Nocturne had escaped!

'What's happening, Frankie?' Gully panted as he ran into the room, before slipping in the slime and careering into a table. 'I heard yelling.'

'More fuss?' Princess Von Tangle popped out of Gully's waistcoat pocket and scowled around the room. 'What now? Can't you lot ever let me have a moment of peace?'

'Impya!' I stammered to my friends. 'She … She's Olympia Nocturne. Cursed mother of my great-great-uncle, Oculus!'

'Ugh! I know!' Viscera moaned. 'It was obvious!'

'What!?' I practically screamed. 'Why didn't you tell me?'

'YOU DIDN'T ASK!' Viscera screamed back. **'PLUS, I WAS FEELING MOODSIE!'**

With that, the minuscule piskie slunk back down into Gully's pocket, muttering to herself.

There was a long moment of shocked silence, as Nancy and Maudlin gathered at the door, along with Calamitus and Tempestra.

'W-w-w-what is it, Bargeous?' Nancy stammered.

'Come now, you eejit,' rasped Maudlin. 'Don't keep us waiting. Did you get her?'

Dad thought for a second before his face hardened into a look of absolute determination.

'If she frees Oculus from his ice prison, we're done for,' he said. 'We don't have any choice but to try and stop her.'

'Should we send a letter to the yetis?' Mum asked nervously.

'It's no use. Goblin postal crows don't fly that far north,' Dad said. I'd never seen him look so serious in all my life. 'Grab all your coats, gloves – every blanket and duvet you can find.'

'Why?' Mum asked. 'I don't understand.'

'Get every warm jumper and pair of socks and scarf as well. ALL OF IT! WE'RE GOING TO THE HIMALAYAS!'

Have you checked out Frankie Banister's other BLUNKiNGLY BONKERS adventures in **The Nothing to See Here Hotel** series?

Steven Butler

Steven B is an award-winning children's writer, actor, voice artist and host of World Book Day's The Biggest Book Show On Earth. When not typing, twirling about on stage, or being very dramatic on screen, Steven spends his time trying to spot thistlewumps at the bottom the garden and catching dust pooks in jars. His *The Wrong Pong* series was shortlisted for the prestigious Roald Dahl Funny Prize.

www.stevenbutlerbooks.com

Steven L is an award-winning illustrator based in Brighton, not far from *The Nothing To See Here Hotel*! As well as designing all of the creatures you have just seen throughout this book, Steven also illustrates the *Shifty McGifty and Slippery Sam* series and Frank Cottrell Boyce's fiction titles. When he isn't drawing giant spiders and geriatric mermaids, Steven loves to eat ice cream on Brighton beach looking out for goblin pirate ships on the horizon.

www.stevenlenton.com

Steven Lenton

is the Patron of Illustration at
Glebe Primary School in East Sussex and set a
competition for the school to design a magical creature
that would feature in this book.

The winner is 'Loucke the Giant Were-Rabbit'
designed by Eloise Manwaring.

Did you spot him on page 179?

Congratulations, Eloise – we love him!

Steven & Steven